Lau...
Dessert

Including
How to Host
Your Own
Vampire
Party!

Laura for DESSERT

Jerry Piasecki

A SKYLARK BOOK

NEW YORK • TORONTO • LONDON • SYDNEY • AUCKLAND

RL5.6, 009–012

LAURA FOR DESSERT
A Skylark Book / October 1995

ISBN 0-553-48285-8

Published simultaneously in the United States and Canada

PRINTED IN THE UNITED STATES OF AMERICA

OPM   0 9 8 7 6 5 4 3 2

Laura for Dessert

PROLOGUE

Laura Easton screamed when she felt something small and furry scurry across her feet. She felt only slightly relieved when she heard it scamper away across the room. Her eyes slowly started to adjust to the darkness that surrounded her. The stone walls of the dungeon in which she had just been placed were dreary, wet, and gray. Laura trembled and almost started to cry. She absolutely hated how she looked in gray.

As more of the cell came into view, Laura realized that the color scheme of her bleak surroundings was the very least of her worries. In the center of the room she noticed what looked like a huge, ancient chopping block made out of the stump of a petrified tree. She saw that portions of the rock walls were scarred with what appeared to be deep claw marks. In one corner the arms of a skeleton dangled from long chains attached to the ceiling. The head and body bones were missing entirely. Laura shivered when she saw that the floor under the skeleton arms was littered with crumpled-up paper plates, plastic straws, used napkins, and a tattered red-checked tablecloth.

The only light in the cell shined dimly through a small, firmly barred window three quarters of the way up one wall and from a small slat halfway up the huge metal door.

Laura looked along the walls for a light switch, which she knew would not be there. What she did find was an old sign with fancy writing on it. The writing was barely visible in the dimness, but after blowing away the dust and moving a tangle of cobwebs, Laura could make out the words:

Welcome to Vanna's Dungeon . . . home of the finest of feasts.

Important Guest Information:
    EMERGENCY EXITS—NONE
    FIRE EXITS—NONE
    CHECKOUT TIME—NONE
    HOPE—NONE
    HAVE A NICE NIGHT!

The words were followed by a smiley face with fangs, and signed:

All the worst,
The Management

Laura Easton knew she was in trouble, deep and serious trouble. Laura Easton had been captured by Vampires, and there was no way out.

CHAPTER

"Daddy!" Laura cried out in panic and fear. Only silence filled the dungeon as her plea echoed off the stone. *"Daaaaaddddddyyyyyyyy!"*

"What is it already? Can't you see I'm, ah, busy?" Horace Easton, Laura's father, carefully poked his head out from behind a stone slab bed in the corner of the cell where he was hiding.

"Daddy." Laura marched up to where her father cowered. "This is all your fault."

"Oh yeah?" Horace said, looking up over his shoulder.

"Yeah."

"Yeah?"

"Yes!" Laura folded her arms and lowered her eyebrows.

Horace decided to stand up for his rights. But when he rose and moved forward, he tripped over the bed and landed on the floor at Laura's feet. He rolled over onto his back and presented his case. "If it's all my fault, then who was the one who said, 'But, Daddy, my teacher is a Vampire'? 'We have to blackmail him,' you said. 'He gave me a D minus minus minus minus minus minus minus,' you said. 'We'll make him change my grade,' you said. 'All we need is proof that he's a Vampire,' you said. 'Let's tell the police,' you said. 'Let's destroy, wreck, and ruin him,' you said."

"And what did you say?" Laura folded her arms.

" 'Okeydokey,' " Horace answered his daughter's question.

"See," Laura said, huffing as only Laura could. "It's all your fault."

Before a single syllable could escape her father's lips, Laura continued. "Now I only have three more words for you, Daddy."

" 'I love you'?" Horace asked hopefully.

"Yeah, right." Laura rolled her eyes. "Try *take me home!* "

"Us too!" Two additional heads popped up from behind the stone slab. They belonged to Sam and Sammi Draper, private eyes whom Horace Easton had hired to get evidence to prove their case and close the casket on Laura's teacher once and for all—or at the very least force him to give Laura an A+++++++.

The Drapers had obtained their evidence in the form of a videotape on which Teacher Vic's image failed to appear. Now the Drapers were destined to share Laura's and Horace's fate as Vampire Lunchables.

Their troubles had begun earlier that night when Vanna, Teacher Vic's former ghoulfriend, overheard the Eastons' plans to deliver the videotape to the police. Vanna and several of her Vampire associates took exception . . . and then took action.

"Look." Laura's dad had poked his daughter in the ribs and giggled as they and the Drapers walked toward the police station with the telltale tape. He pointed to seven caped figures moving swiftly toward them through the shadows. "Those people are dressed just like your teacher."

Horace was about to discover that the figures had much more in common with Teacher Vic than a shared sense of style. As soon as the two groups met, the humans had found themselves surrounded by a sudden whirlwind of capes.

As the Vampires moved faster and faster around their prey, Laura felt as though she were in some sort of black tornado; Horace and Sam Draper were too terrified to speak, and all Sammi kept screaming was "I want to go bowling! I really want to go bowling!"

As Sammi continued to shriek, a female face

emerged from the dark, swirling mass that surrounded the group. The face leaned in a little more until it was nose to nose with Sammi. Then it bared its dripping fangs.

"Bowling?" The Vampire smiled. "What a wonderful idea. I think I have just the right bowl to fit you at home." The Vampire licked her already wet lips.

"Come back, Vanna." A gravelly voice snarled from the cyclone. "We need your help carrying these groceries."

"I'm sorry to tease," she said, giggling in Sammi's ear while nipping at the lobe. "I could never resist playing with my food." Vanna threw her head back and laughed.

As soon as Vanna disappeared back into the swirl, Horace Easton, Laura, and the Drapers felt themselves being lifted up into the air. They rose swiftly and started to spin.

All became a twirling, twisting blur until they landed with four mighty bumps in the dismal dungeon in which they currently resided.

"How am I supposed to 'take you home'?" Mr. Easton asked, mimicking Laura's plea. "Maybe I should just call a cab."

"Cool," Sammi Draper said. "Dibs on the window seat."

Laura stomped angrily over to the door, stood on her toes, and peeked through the small slat. It took her a moment to figure out what she was seeing, but then it dawned on her. The cupboards, the counters, the sink, the stove . . . Next to the dungeon was a kitchen! And standing right in the middle of that kitchen was the Vampire whom the voice in the whirlwind had called Vanna.

Vanna was wearing a black apron. Her raven-black hair was pulled back in a bun, and she was on the phone. Laura couldn't help noticing how absolutely beautiful Vanna looked in the candlelit kitchen. Her gray-green eyes flashed, reflecting the flames. Her skin was as white as the full moon, and her gestures reminded Laura of a cat at play.

Laura was almost hypnotized by the sight of Vanna, until the Vampire let out a peal of wicked laughter and Laura felt her whole body shiver. While Vanna was perhaps one of the most beautiful creatures Laura had ever seen, she could also sense that Vanna was completely, totally, and unashamedly evil —a quality that had made Vanna the most popular girl ever to attend Vampire High.

Laura took a deep breath and listened as Vanna spoke into the phone in a voice as smooth as melted caramel. From the cell she heard the Vampire laugh and joke with caterers, party planners, and invitation printers. Laura could tell that Vanna was about to throw a big dinner party and that she wanted to make sure everything was just so.

Meanwhile, back in the realm of the living, none of Laura's fellow sixth-graders had the slightest inkling of the dangers their friend now faced. That fateful night while Laura, her father, and the dippy Drapers were becoming human tornadoes, the rest of Laura's classmates had been across town also in danger. Laura had sent them to Teacher Vic's house to keep him busy while she took her evidence to the police. But Teacher Vic had chosen to live in the worst neighborhood in town. (It reminded him so much of home.) And as the students had walked down their teacher's street, they'd been surrounded by a gang of goons who were up to no good. It looked as if the Lincolnview sixth grade was about to become an endangered species, when a guardian Vampire came to the rescue.

When it was all over, Teacher Vic had been forced to reveal his true identity to save his students. He'd been ready to hang up his chalk and return to the family business, but Peter, Amanda, Amy, Gabe, Alan, Mary, and the rest of the class had helped him change his mind. They'd convinced Vic that they had no problem with having a teacher who was a Vampire—as long as he was a *retired* Vampire.

Monday turned out to be pretty much learning as usual in Room 113. The classroom itself appeared exactly as it had the previous Friday. All the window shades remained nailed shut to block out every ray of sunshine. The light switches were still fixed with Super Glue in the Off position. Candelabras were blazing by the blackboard.

In fact by all appearances it would have been difficult to tell that anything had changed in Room 113 of the Lincolnview School if it hadn't been for Teacher Vic's mouth. He no longer hid his mouth when he smiled or tried to conceal his fangs when he laughed—and right at that moment he was grinning from fang to shining fang.

Teacher Vic was in a wonderful mood. Now that he could be himself and be proud of it, he felt as if a three-million-pound stone had been taken off his shoulders. In fact, he was so happy that he started the day by announcing a surprise spelling test. Peter was thoroughly underwhelmed.

"*Scream,*" Teacher Vic said to his students.

Peter obliged. "*Arrrrgggggghhhhhhh!*"

"Come on, Peter," Teacher Vic said. "Spell it, don't tell it."

Peter looked around for Laura for a little teacher-tormenting support, and when he didn't see her, he thought how lucky she was to be missing the quiz.

"*Screech*." Teacher Vic read the second word on his list and looked at Peter. "Don't even think it."

Overall Peter was a very good student. He was just a horrible speller. He sighed and wrote *s-c-r-e-a-s-h* on his paper.

"*Scary*." Teacher Vic read the next word.

"You're telling me," Peter said as he wrote *s-k-a-r-y* on his paper.

Teacher Vic wasn't bothered by Peter's antics. Everything was as it should be. Even the class mascots, Lester the parrot and Frances the firefly, were back from their trip to the mountains. Lester and Frances were Teacher Vic's friends and helpers. They had been with him for centuries, and he was glad to have them back. Besides, he was having too great a time thinking up his favorite words for the spelling test to let anything get to him. Words he loved to say and those that brought back fond memories of his childhood.

"Shriek." Teacher Vic giggled. "Don't you all just adore spelling tests?"

"You want the truth?" Peter asked.

"No."

"Love 'em."

Laura's would-be boyfriend, Donny, sat quietly at the back of the room. He had been with Laura, her dad, and the Drapers for part of Friday evening and was somewhat surprised to see Teacher Vic back on the job. Laura's empty desk also confused him. He sat there looking and feeling puzzled and a little scared. But since Donny often had a look of fearful confusion on his face, no one paid much attention.

"Shish ka-Bobby." Teacher Vic laughed out loud and showed his teeth again. "Just kidding." He tried to regain control when he noticed that no one else was laughing.

It had also struck Teacher Vic as a little odd that morning that Laura was absent and no one had called in. But he knew her parents were divorced and that she lived with her father—and that her father was Horace Easton and that Horace Easton could easily forget to call. Most of the rest of the class thought Laura was either sick or skipping. It wouldn't have been the first time.

"Last two words." Teacher Vic smiled. "*Savage* and *supper*. Extra-credit word: *suck*."

When Laura was still not in class on Tuesday, Teacher Vic and his students became concerned. By Wednesday they were downright worried. Then, on Thursday, everyone heard the news on the radio or TV. Horace Easton; his twelve-year-old daughter, Laura; and two private detectives named the Drapers had mysteriously disappeared.

CHAPTER

"Did you hear what happened?" Peter said on Thursday morning as he walked up to his friends, who were waiting outside school for the bell to ring. "This is really scary." Each student who had joined the group had said the same thing. Every radio, TV station, and newspaper carried the story.

"Police have no clues as to their whereabouts," a reporter on WFS Radio said.

VANISHED WITHOUT A TRACE, the newspaper headline read.

"Laura Easton to marry three-headed crab-boy from Atlantis. Father and private eyes dive into ocean and shout 'Eureka!'" the TV talk shows reported. One of them even had a panel of people who said that they too were married to Atlantians. Several of those on the panel claimed to be growing gills.

"My sister believes what she hears on those talk

shows," Peter said. "But then again, she *is* a three-headed crab."

"Would you do me a favor?" Amanda put her hand on Peter's shoulder.

"What?" Peter was excited. He was secretly starting to like Amanda . . . a little.

"Shut up."

Peter's excitement melted away faster than a Fudgsicle in a forest fire.

"Look." Amy pointed down toward the other end of the school building. "Maybe he knows something."

The object of Amy's point, Donny, waved and ran up to his classmates. "Did you hear what happened?" Donny sounded about fifty percent worried and fifty percent scared.

"That's what we want you to tell us," Gabe said. "What *did* happen Friday night?"

"I don't know." Donny shrugged.

"Earth to Donny. Come in, Donny." Amy rapped Donny on the forehead with her knuckles. "You did go with Laura and her dad to meet the Drapers, right?"

"Yeah."

"So . . ."

"So, what?" Donny was getting a bit defensive. "Look, all I know is that while you guys were being rescued by that teacher, we were on our way to the police station with a videotape proving that Teacher Vic is a Vampire."

"What was on that video?" Amanda asked.

"Nothing," Donny answered.

"How did 'nothing' prove he was a Vampire?" Amy asked.

"Because when I say nothing, I mean nothing. The Drapers videoed Teacher Vic in his house, but when we looked at the tape, he wasn't there. His school ring and stuff were there, all moving around in the air by themselves, but Teacher Vic wasn't."

After a moment of nervous silence, Peter asked, "What happened then?"

"Then, when we were almost to the police station, I remembered that my parents said they'd vaporize me, and then ground me, if I was home late. So Laura's dad dropped me off, and away they went."

"Have you told any of this to the police?" Mary asked.

"No."

"Have you told any of this to Teacher Vic?" Peter asked.

"Double no."

Peter looked at Amy, who said, "Well, we think you'd better."

"Are you all a bunch of Froot Loops?" Donny protested. "I can't tell Teacher Vic what we were going to do. I like my blood right where it is, on the inside of me. That guy is a Vampire."

"A retired Vampire," everyone corrected.

A moment later the bell rang. Gabe and Alan each took one of Donny's elbows, lifted him up, and carried him into school.

"We think Donny has something to say to you," Amanda said as Gabe and Alan plopped their wiggling friend down right in front of the teacher's candlelit desk.

Teacher Vic threw his cape back over his shoulders and stared at Donny with his catlike steel-gray eyes. "So? You want to talk?"

"Not really." Donny tried to turn away, but his friends turned him back.

"You're not afraid of me, are you?" Vic sounded normal, but any illusion of normality quickly vanished when he floated up off his chair and across his desk. He hovered about a foot off the ground right in front of Donny.

Most of the people in class took a step back. Several gulped, and one squeaked.

"What's wrong?" Teacher Vic asked as he settled down to the ground.

"Ah, nothing." Peter's voice sounded only a little

shaky. "It's just that having a floating teacher is going to take some getting used to."

"Oh, sorry," Vic said. "Ancient habits are hard to break."

Teacher Vic then walked behind his desk and sat down. He immediately got up and this time walked around the desk so that he ended up once again in front of Donny. This time Teacher Vic's feet stayed firmly on the ground. "How's that?" he asked Peter.

"Much better, thanks."

"No problem," Vic said casually. "Now, let's hear what Donald has to say."

"Yeah, come on, Donny," Gabe said. "Tell him."

Everyone in class joined in a chorus of encouragement. Donny felt he had no choice but to speak. After he'd told everything that had happened, from Laura's plans to the Drapers' video, Teacher Vic moaned. "I can't believe Laura would do that to me."

Then Teacher Vic's sadness took a quick turn, becoming total embarrassment. "I can't believe the Drapers *could* do that to me."

"Why didn't they see you on the videotape?" Amy asked.

Teacher Vic shook his head and shrugged. "I just never photographed well. I mean, I never photographed at all. It's like that old reflection-in-the-mirror business—Vampires just don't show up on film, or tape."

Amy had a very thoughtful look on her face. "If you don't have any pictures of yourself," she said slowly, choosing her words carefully, "and you can't ever see your reflection . . ."

Amy paused until Teacher Vic said, "Yes?"

"Then how do you know what you look like?"

Everyone could tell that Teacher Vic was taken aback by Amy's question. "I guess I don't know what I look like."

"Doesn't that drive you nuts?" Amy asked.

"It didn't . . . until now." Teacher Vic stomped his feet. "Thanks a heap, Amy. Wait until *your* next report card."

Teacher Vic sounded very serious, but he was smiling. His smile grew even broader when Amanda came to her friend's rescue. "Maybe we could all draw your picture."

"Terrific!" Everyone clearly heard Teacher Vic clap, although no one saw his hands move. "I think this is my good side." Teacher Vic turned to his right. "Or is this my good side?" He quickly turned to his left. "Does a Vampire even have a good side? So many questions still to be answered. But first I have some teaching to do, you have some learning to accomplish, and then we all have a mystery to solve."

After an easy quiz, a boring lecture on parrot politics by Lester, silent reading time, and lunch, Teacher Vic launched into the discussion on the subject that had stayed on everyone's mind all morning long. What might have happened to Laura, her dad, and the Drapers?

"Does anyone have any ideas?" he asked.

Donny was the first to raise his hand. He had spent the most time with Mr. Easton and knew him better than anyone else in the class, except Laura. Donny knew exactly the kind of person Laura's dad was. Therefore, he suggested that Mr. Easton might have gotten lost on the way to the police station and ended up out of gas somewhere in rural New Jersey. Everyone agreed that it was a very definite possibility.

Other explanations for the disappearances ranged from thousand-foot-deep potholes to Walt Disney World vacations. No one even came close to guessing what had really happened, including Teacher Vic. Now that he knew Laura was with her dad, he was sure she would soon be back in class and that everything would work out fine. (Ever since he first had baby fangs, Vic had been a most optimistic and cheery Vampire. It drove his parents nuts.)

Teacher Vic remained optimistic about Laura's return until later that evening, when, on his way home from work, he decided to drop by the Drapers' house to see if they'd come home.

Teacher Vic looked up the Drapers' address in the phone book. When he arrived at their house, he found that the front door was locked tight, but the big picture window to its right had been blown out into about a zillion tiny pieces. From all the glass on the grass and sidewalk, it was clear that the window had been shattered from the inside.

Teacher Vic checked carefully for nosy neighbors before flying through the opening and coming in for an abrupt landing in the Drapers' living room. He slowly turned around and carefully sniffed the air. "Vanna," he whispered. "What have you done?"

Teacher Vic could still smell Vanna's perfume. It was faint, but it was definitely there. The scent of Blood No. 5 was unmistakably in the air. Vic sighed, remembering that Vanna was always sure to put a drop of A positive behind each ear and on her right wrist before raiding a village or terrifying a town.

But this was no time to think about the good old

days. It was obvious that Vanna had visited the Drapers. It was even more obvious that she'd been very, very angry when she'd left.

The CD player was flattened, the VCR was crushed into a ball, and the furniture was splintered. Vic saw deep grooves dug into one wall where Vanna had slashed long, thick ribbons of plaster away with her nails. If Teacher Vic listened really hard, he thought he could still hear Vanna's shrieks of anger.

Gee, Vic thought. *Vanna hasn't been this mad since I forgot her thirteen hundredth birthday. This doesn't look good.*

Things looked a whole lot worse for Laura and company when Teacher Vic got home. Waiting for him on his dining room table was an engraved invitation. It read,

You are cordially invited to attend Vanna's dinner party.

> **TIME:** Midnight
> **DAY:** Saturday
> **PLACE:** Vanna's castle
> **DRESS:** Black cape required

Under the engraved letters was a handwritten note from Vanna:

22

Victorio, darling,

I do hope you come. I believe you know everyone who will be there, including the meal itself.

Come home, dearest, and enjoy the feast.

Love, Vanna

CHAPTER

Teacher Vic was a wreck. He knew he had a big problem. Granted, it wasn't as big as Laura's, but it was pretty darn big. When he'd chosen to save his class from the street gang, only his cover and his job had been at stake. Now his very nature was on the line. While he *had* retired from active Vampiring, he had no desire to donate his fangs to science. He was proud of his Vampire heritage; he just didn't care for it as a profession.

Vic knew what any self-respecting Vampire would do. What any Vampire with even the tiniest shred of living-dead dignity or lick of demonic decency would decide. If it were a question on a test in Sunnight school, the answer would be easy: Get your cape cleaned, polish your fangs, and work up a hearty appetite.

Vanna was famous for her dinner parties. She usually hired only the best caterers in the Vampire Kingdom. Expensive caterers such as Barry's Bloodmobile and Munchies, Nick's Necks & Noshes, or Wally's We Truck-um, You Suck-um. For this party she might even go all out and book the best: Curley Red's Blood Vessels. The thought was enough to make Teacher Vic's mouth water and his stomach growl so loudly that his neighbors thought they had a bear in the basement.

Teacher Vic understood that any Vampire worth her or his hemoglobin would simply live for an invitation. He also understood that he should be very honored to attend.

But how could he stand by and let one of his students become dinner, no matter how fancy the party might be? If he wanted to teach humans, Vic knew he just couldn't consume them. He needed some advice, so he turned to his top advisers, Lester the parrot and Frances the firefly.

After several minutes, during which time they carefully considered the situation, Frances blinked out, and Lester very thoughtfully said, "Let 'em fry."

"What?" Teacher Vic asked loudly.

A tiny voice echoed, "What?" Frances flickered slightly as she spoke.

"Or boil, or bake, or broil, or whatever Vanna's caterers have in mind. Let them serve Laura tartare if they want. No skin off my beak."

Laura tartare. Teacher Vic thought about it for a moment and then overruled his appetite. "I don't think we can let that happen."

"Of course we can let that happen," Lester squawked. "You know you can't save another Vampire's food before he or she becomes leftovers. It's the First Law. Besides, look what that Laura and her dad were going to do to you. What creeps! What lowlifes! What scum-sucking liver slimes! What . . ."

As Lester ran down his list of insulting names, Teacher Vic nodded and sighed. He knew only too well that the first lesson any young Vampire learns is: There's no such thing as a *freed* lunch. Anyone who let a person who was destined for a Vampire's palate go free had to suffer the consequences. No one was sure what those consequences were, because no Vampire had ever broken the First Law. And when it comes to Vampires, *ever* is a very long time. Vic remembered a nursery rhyme he learned at his first night-care center:

> Break the law and you will see
> what it's like to truly be
> flesh and blood, skin and bones,
> all the lunches you have known.
> Don't be dumb, don't be crude.
> Yes, be nasty and be rude.

Suck their blood, don't set them free,
or doomed to dust you'll surely be.

Teacher Vic knew that the rhyme was supposed to scare Vampire pups so that they would never even think of breaking V.K. Law 1. Now, even though it had been centuries since he learned it, the rhyme still sent a shiver up Teacher Vic's spine.

On the other hand Vic figured that "Don't let anyone drink your students' blood, regardless of their behavior" just had to be one of the top ten rules of teaching humans.

"I hate to agree with Lester." Frances's tiny voice was so soft that it was next to impossible to hear what she was saying unless you were real close or happened to have a Vampire's supersensitive hearing. "But if you save them, it will be lights out for you." Frances dimmed her light to dramatize her point. "Face it, my fangy-faced friend. You just can't do it."

Lester tilted his head from one side to the other as only a parrot can. He couldn't make out a word Frances had just said, but he was sure it was about him and that it was not the least bit complimentary. "What'd she say about me? What'd she say?" Lester and Frances had always been quite competitive. "Can't you get that little fleabag to speak up so that normal birds can hear her?"

Frances, as would any proud firefly, hated being called a flea. She buzzed words that Vic had had no idea she knew. She then flew up and started circling Lester's head, making him very dizzy.

When Teacher Vic left the room, Frances was circling the parrot's head at the speed of sound and Lester was snapping wildly at the wind with his beak. While it was true that Frances spoke very softly, Teacher Vic had heard every word she'd said. She wasn't wrong, but what she said also just wasn't right.

Vic glided over to his telephone. He really needed someone he could talk to . . . some professional advice. Teacher Vic dialed a telephone number that he'd seen on a billboard back home in the V.K. The number, 123-BITE, had been easy to remember because the last four digits matched the radio station's call letters.

After several rings a male voice answered and said, "Good evening. Thank you for calling BITE Radio. Just hang on the line. You'll be next to talk with Dr. Revenant."

"Please hurry," Vic said before being put on hold. "I'm calling *very* long distance."

BITE was the talk radio station in the V.K. Dr. Julie Revenant had a show five nights a week. Vampires from all over the kingdom called to talk about their problems and hopefully get some help. Usually the problems were pretty simple: boy-Vampire/girl-Vampire stuff, fear of flying, trouble changing into a rodent, Elvis sightings, things like that. Vic's problem was a bit more complex.

After listening to the show over the telephone for a couple of minutes, Vic heard Dr. Revenant wrapping up the previous call. "So remember, in the V.K. there's a sucker born every minute."

Vic heard her click off that line and click onto his. "Hello, you're on with Dr. Revenant. How's death treating you?" The good doctor waited for Vic to start talking about his problem.

Teacher Vic put his cape in front of his mouth and spoke in a high, squeaky voice to hide his identity.

Dr. Revenant was known as one of the most sympathetic and helpful Vampire radio psychologists in the V.K. She never failed to give wonderful advice to her callers. The radio station advertised her program by labeling her "the vampire with a heart." Indeed in her full-color newspaper ads Dr. Revenant looked caring and concerned, and the heart she held in her hands appeared to be still beating.

Dr. Revenant listened patiently as Vic told her the entire story. When he was done, there was total silence for a second or two. Then she responded carefully, thoughtfully, and sincerely to Vic's problem. "You're sick, dude! Totally wacko!"

Teacher Vic could actually feel her anger bubbling and growing through the telephone line. He started to regret having placed the call.

"Sick! Sick! Sick! You want to save humans? Are you crazy? Of course you're crazy! Who are you? What's your name? We'll have your cape for this! Your fangs! Your—"

Teacher Vic had heard enough. He hung up the phone sadly. His decision had certainly not been made any easier. He still had two choices. He could call Vanna and say *"Bon appétit,"* or he could break his bloodline and try to save his student.

Vic sat down on the edge of his couch and sighed deeply. "Boy, this teaching business is really, really, *really* tough."

CHAPTER

As Teacher Vic struggled to make his choice, Laura wrestled with the realization that she had no choices at all. As hard as she thought, she just couldn't think of a way out of the cell. Through the slat in the dungeon door she watched Vanna at her kitchen table. Laura's Vampire captor read cookbook after cookbook, trying to decide what recipes to suggest to her caterers. From where she stood, Laura could just barely read the titles of some of the books: titles such as *The Way to a Man's Heart Is Through His Stomach: A Diner's Guide* and *The Good Castlekeeping Women's Cookbook: Human Females for Vampires on the Go.*

Laura watched as Vanna read hundreds of recipes. When Vanna thought one looked particularly delicious, she'd tear out the page, look over at the dungeon door, and laugh. When she caught sight of

Laura through the slat, she laughed all the more loudly and licked her lips.

"Decisions, decisions, decisions." Vanna winked at Laura through the slat and closed the last cookbook.

By Thursday morning Teacher Vic had made his decision and packed his bag. The one thing he didn't expect to have was traveling companions.

"I'm going with you," Peter said as soon as Teacher Vic had told the class what had happened to Laura, her dad, and the Drapers, and that he intended to rescue them.

"You're what?" Teacher Vic was shocked by Peter's announcement.

"I said I'm going with you," Peter repeated slowly.

"Me too," Amanda said.

"Me three," Amy joined in.

"Me five." Donny raised his hand. "Ahhhhh, I mean four."

By the time the class got to me's number sixteen and seventeen, Teacher Vic proclaimed, "Enough!" He spoke with such force that everyone else stopped talking. "You don't know what you're saying. This journey is not going to be some sort of picnic. You know, like falling off the Empire State Building while wearing concrete high-tops. This journey is *really* dangerous. Dangerous beyond your wildest imagination or most frightening nightmare. This is even more dangerous than eating the Meat Loaf and Lima Bean Surprise in the lunchroom."

Everyone gasped.

"Okay," Teacher Vic continued. "Maybe it's not *that* dangerous, but what is?"

After a moment of silence in memory of all those who had unknowingly or accidentally eaten lunchroom lima beans, Gabe said, "Teacher Vic, you have to let us help."

"Yeah!" everyone yelled.

"You might need us," Peter said. "We could help you find them, or keep a lookout, or—"

"Or end up as twelve-year-old Pop-Tarts," Teacher Vic said, finishing Peter's statement.

"No way," Amanda joked. "Student strudel— maybe. Pop-Tarts? Never!"

While her classmates laughed, Amanda's teacher moaned. "Hel-lo, people. Let's get real, shall we?" Teacher Vic had been standing in front of the class; now he was behind it.

He stood next to Lester's cage. "Lester," Teacher Vic said. "Would you please tell our friends what they say about humans in the V.K.?"

"Oh," Lester said. "You mean about how silly they

look when they try to button and zip up their blue jeans after they've been shrunk in the wash?"

"No, the other thing," Vic said.

"Oh," Lester squawked. "You mean, 'Good to the last drop.' "

Everyone had turned to look at Teacher Vic, but as soon as they did, he was back in front of the class. "So unless your goal in life is to become a menu item, I suggest you all stay put."

"Stay put" was the exact order Vanna had given Laura, Horace Easton, and the Drapers the night before as she danced into the cell carrying a golden tray holding things called Quarter Pounders, Big Macs, Chicken McNuggets, and french fries.

After putting away her cookbooks, Vanna had flown these human delicacies in all the way from Duluth. It was the twenty-third meal Vanna had served her dinner. Previously she had imported other items that she hadn't recognized by sight, smell, or name. Strange things such as Whoppers, Frosties, hot dogs, bacon cheeseburgers, and the strangest of all . . . double-bean burritos.

To Vanna's Vampire eyes this material didn't look even close to edible. But her own food seemed to enjoy it, particularly the courses called the Drapers and Horace Easton. Vanna felt that their smiles made her efforts worthwhile. After all, she wanted all her meals to be happy meals.

"Eat heartily, my tasty little yummikins," Vanna said when she put down the tray of McTreats. "Soon I'll bring dessert."

"Promise?" Sammi trembled with delight.

"Cross your heart and hope you die." Vanna crossed Sammi's heart with her index finger. Her nail cut a perfect X in his shirt.

"Good." Sammi ran for the food. "Dessert is the most important meal of the day."

The Drapers and Horace always wolfed down their food as soon as Vanna delivered it. Laura just nibbled around the edges and glared angrily whenever Vanna entered the dungeon.

Vanna thought the girl was rude, ungrateful, and totally lacking in social graces. Vanna was impressed. She thought that had Laura been a Vampire instead of human, they might actually almost have been friends.

The next day in Room 113 at Lincolnview School, Teacher Vic covered his ears to block out the sound of all of his students whining the word *Pleeeeeease* at the same time.

"For the last time, you can't come," Teacher Vic moaned as he glided nervously back and forth in front of the class. The fact that his feet were at least an inch and a half above the floor no longer seemed out of the ordinary.

"For the last time, you have to let us come," Amy said.

"For the last time, why?" Teacher Vic thought about pulling on his hair for dramatic effect. But then he remembered that he was already getting a bit thin on top and that his grandVamp had been almost completely bald by the time he was four thousand.

"Because she's our *friend*," Amy said.

Teacher Vic paused. He hadn't expected Amy's answer. The human concept of true friendship was something he didn't quite understand, but he did respect it. Vampire friendships can last centuries and still end over a single drop of B negative. After more than several uncomfortably silent moments, during which Teacher Vic searched for a way to say no, he said, "Yes."

"But you have to let us come—" Peter stopped midwhine. "Yes?"

"Yes."

"Yes!" about half the class shouted in unison while the other half slapped high fives in celebration.

Everyone started making travel plans at once. So many people were talking at the same time that no single person, or Vampire, could be heard above the crowd.

To get his class's attention, Teacher Vic waved his cape, causing a loud peal of thunder to crash through the room and a bolt of scarlet lightning to streak through the air.

When everyone stopped screaming and caught their breath, Peter simply said, "Cool. Can you teach us to do that?"

"Maybe next grading period," Teacher Vic said as he got back to the subject at hand. "I hate to disappoint you, but—"

"Ahhh, man," Gabe moaned. "I knew it. He might be a Vampire, but he's still a grown-up. See, he's going to change his mind."

"No, I'm not."

"You mean we can all still go with you?" Gabe asked suspiciously.

"No."

"Grown-up."

"There's no need to be insulting, Gabriel. When I said yes, I didn't mean everyone could come."

"But *some* of us can still come?" Alan asked.

"Well, yes." Teacher Vic made some quick calculations before continuing. "But no more than five, or we'll stand out like a sore artery."

"Which five?" Donny asked.

"That's up to you," Teacher Vic said. "Whoever you select must meet me in the playground at eight tomorrow morning."

"But that's after the sun comes up," Gabe said.

"That's right."

"But I thought that Vampires turned to glop or Silly Putty or something in the sun," Amy said.

"That's true, if we're in the sunshine for more than a few minutes. But once we're in the V.K., I'm sure I'd have more chance of survival in the light than any of you would have after dark." Teacher Vic sat down at his desk. "Besides, going during the day will give us a chance to rescue Laura and the rest while most of the Vampires are still asleep."

"What if we wake them?" Amy asked.

No one felt very comfortable when Teacher Vic couldn't come up with an answer.

In Vanna's dungeon Laura still had absolutely no idea how she was going to avoid becoming a Vampire Big Gulp. She did know that she needed to come up with something fast because, judging from Vanna's giddy mood, it was clear that time was running out.

CHAPTER

After school that Friday the students met near the swings to decide who was to go and who would stay behind. Several students had to take themselves out of the competition. One had a dentist's appointment, three others had birthday parties, and five had soccer practice.

That left thirteen students. "Talk about a lucky number," Peter said half joking. "I guess things can't get much worse now."

Just as Peter completed his sentence, a large black cat scampered through the group, and Amanda dropped her pocket mirror, which shattered on contact with the cement.

"Maybe it's Opposite Day," Amanda said slowly, "and all these things mean good luck."

"I hope you're right," Peter said. "Let's draw for it."

Amy had torn a large piece of paper into thirteen

little pieces. She put them into her Georgetown Hoyas baseball cap. On five of the pieces she had written the word *blood*. On the remaining pieces she'd written *skin*. Those who drew *blood* would be the ones to go with Teacher Vic. The winners were Gabe, Amanda, Donny, Peter, and Amy. Everyone congratulated the five, who suddenly weren't sure whether they should celebrate their victory or write out their wills.

While her friends walked home from the playground, Laura waited for darkness and for Vanna. At the request of Sammi Draper, Vanna had promised her future food a breakfast of pancakes, pork rinds, potato chips, and peanut brittle. It was Sammi's favorite breakfast, which explained the ever-increasing bulge of his belly and his many bouts with world-class indigestion.

The Drapers and Laura's dad were as frightened as could be, but they never let it dampen their appetites. Vanna was always on time, if not early, with their meals. These two facts gave Laura an idea, and a plan of escape.

"Are you sure you know what to do?" she asked Sammi for the fifteenth time.

"No problem," Sammi said as he patted his growling stomach. "Just remember, I get your pork rinds."

The last thing Teacher Vic wanted that night was visitors, but visitors he got. Vic had barely returned home when his whole family slowly drifted down through the ceiling. Everyone wore their usual black flying capes to match their hair and to contrast with their almost pure-white skin. Vic's sister, Vivian, wore a bright red scrunchie in her ponytail.

"Sorry to drop in without calling first," Vic's dad said. "We just happened to be flying through the area and thought we'd float by and see if you were home."

"Oh, yeah, like, right." Vic was amazed at how much he was starting to sound like his students. "You always hang out this far away from home."

"What do we hang out this far from home?" Vic's dad sounded confused.

"You have cable?" Vivian settled onto the couch while his brother, Vinnie, opened and rummaged through the refrigerator.

"Hey, Fang." Vinnie used the nickname Vic hated while he pushed a bottle of ketchup off a shelf and tossed a pitcher of tomato juice across the room. "Don't you got anyone to eat in this place?"

"You just ate an hour ago," their mom scolded.

"Exactly my point," Vinnie said. "I'm starving. Can we grab a bite on the way home?"

"If we see someone convenient." Their mom

turned toward Vic and shook her head. "It's as if your brother never sank his teeth into a neck before. He's always hungry."

"Hey, Fang!" Vinnie yelled. "Why do you keep all this junk in here?" Vinnie had opened the freezer part of Vic's fridge. He tossed six TV dinners, some fish sticks, a box of microwave fries, a frozen cherry pie, and a carton of strawberry ice cream onto the floor. "Why no food? Don't humans pay their teachers enough to eat on?"

Vic raced over and put all the things back into the freezer. "This *is* food." He pushed Vinnie out of the way.

"Well, don't invite me for dinner." Vinnie laughed.

"Don't worry, I won't." Teacher Vic glared at his brother.

"Speaking of dinner"—their mom stepped between her sons—"we brought a gift for you, Victor."

Vic's dad reached behind his back and brought forward a big, beautifully wrapped box. It was covered with shiny black paper and red ribbons, Vic's favorite color combination. "Go on, son." Vic's dad handed him the box. "Open it."

When Vic pulled the lid off the box, he found it contained the most stunningly stylish formal dinner cape he'd ever seen.

"Try it on," Vivian said. "It's from Capers, no less." Vivian spoke in a very snooty voice. "It's what all the best Vampires are wearing."

"Sure," Vinnie said sarcastically as he again started throwing things out of his brother's freezer. "Give it to the Vampire who lives with humans. Give it to the teacher, the veggie-breath carrot-cruncher."

"Vincent," his mother interrupted, "watch your language! What have I told you about swearing?"

"It's just not fair!" Vinnie pointed at Vic. "The granola-head gets a cape from Capers. Me? I get a pair of black jeans from the Gasp."

"I thought you said you wanted a pair of Gasp jeans, jerk-jaw," Vivian said.

"I did want them," Vinnie said. "But now I want a cape from Capers. It's *no fair*!"

"No one ever said living death would be fair," his dad said.

"Well, just remember that I didn't ask to be dead," Vinnie responded.

"Never mind about your brother, Victor." Their mom smiled at her youngest son. "Just try on the cape and see how it flies."

Vic stuck his tongue out at Vinnie and threw the cape over his shoulders. "What do you think?" Vic modeled the cape in front of his family.

"VMTV all the way." Vivian clapped her hands. Telling someone they looked like they could be on Vampire Music Television was Vic's sister's biggest compliment.

Vic's dad circled his son and nodded approvingly. Vic's mom ran up to him and kissed him on the cheek. "Perfect! It's absolutely perfect! You'll be the talk of the party."

"What party?" Vic asked suspiciously.

"Vanna's dinner party, of course," Vic's mom said casually. "Tomorrow night? You did get your invitation, didn't you?"

Reluctantly Teacher Vic took off the cape, folded it, and carefully placed it back in the box. He handed the box to his dad. "Nice try," he said. "But I've decided that I will not have one of my students for dinner."

"I can't understand why not." Vic's father sounded surprised. "You have so many of them."

"I can't drink Laura," Teacher Vic said. "If for no other reason than that the PTA would go crazy."

"You don't have to have any Laura if you don't want to," Vic's mother said kindly. "There will be plenty of blood to go around. Vanna's having the caterers serve all four. She phoned and said she's fattening them up in celebration of what she hopes will be your homecoming. Vanna even promised that you could have the honor of making the first puncture."

"Sure. Fine. Now *he* gets first puncture." Vinnie slammed a box of sugar-free Popsicles onto the floor and stomped on it with both feet.

"Would you please grow up?" Vivian snapped. "You're such a baby bat sometimes. Sheesh!"

In a puff of gray smoke Vinnie transformed himself into a bat wearing diapers and chased his sister out of the room.

Vic and his parents looked at each other in deathly silence. When he hadn't said a word for more than a minute, Vic's parents knew that their son, even with the promise of first puncture, was not about to change his mind.

"I guess we should be going," Vic's mom said softly. Her disappointment was clear.

"I'm sorry, Mom," was all Teacher Vic could say. "I'm really sorry."

"We are too," Vic's dad said. "Vincent! Vivian! Stop playing. We're leaving."

Vivian floated into the room holding a diapered bat between her teeth.

"Vivian," her mom said, "get your brother out of your mouth. You don't know where he's been."

As soon as Vivian spat, Vinnie returned to his original form. "You didn't have to bite." Vinnie tried to regain some shred of his dignity. "But you know, of course, that I let you catch me."

Vivian snarled, revealing her fangs. Vinnie backed away quickly and stood behind his dad.

Vic's father nodded to the rest. With that the entire family started to leave the way it had arrived, by floating through the ceiling. When only their feet were still visible, Teacher Vic heard Vinnie say, "If he doesn't want it, can I keep the cape?"

Vic couldn't make out his father's reply, but he certainly heard Vinnie shout, "You what?" just before the soles of their shoes moved through the ceiling and his family was gone.

Teacher Vic breathed a sigh of relief. Then he looked down and saw the box. Vic picked it up and smiled. On the box cover he read the words CAPERS, FOR FEASTS MOST FORMAL.

Meanwhile in Vanna's dungeon, Laura excitedly paced back and forth and cracked her knuckles. She was sure her escape plan would work, and she wouldn't even let herself think about what would happen if it didn't.

CHAPTER

That night Vanna was in a most glorious mood. She hadn't felt so good in centuries. This was going to be her most spectacular dinner party yet, and she was beside herself with joy. Vanna had decided to spare no expense and had selected Curley Red's Blood Vessels to cater the feast. She was expecting Curley to arrive at any moment to discuss the menu and select the side dishes. Vanna absolutely adored Curley Red's clotted noodle soup, and his plasma punch was without equal.

Vanna arranged the pork rinds in the shape of a heart around a stack of pancakes, picked up the tray, and floated off to feed her livestock.

Sammi was keeping watch through the dungeon door when Vanna made her appearance in the kitchen. As soon as he noticed her approaching the cell, he started jumping up and down like a dog at dinnertime.

Sam Draper whapped his brother upside the head. When Sammi didn't seem to notice, Sam did it again. "Shhh, doodle-brain," Sam said. "Just remember the plan."

"Oh yeah." Sammi rubbed his head. "The plan."

Meanwhile Vanna unlocked the cell door, opened it, and drifted in. "Hello, my sweets." She smiled her very fangy smile. "Don't we look scrumptious today."

"Now!" Laura yelled.

Instantly each Draper jumped into action, grabbing one of Vanna's arms and holding on tight. Laura's dad dove for and grabbed the Vampire's legs with all his might.

Vanna seemed quite amused. "Aren't we the hungry little snack cakes," she said with a laugh. "You couldn't even wait for me to put it down?" Despite the fact that she had a Draper on each arm, Vanna held the tray perfectly straight and steady.

"Yes, my morsels, tonight you shall eat, drink, and be merry . . ." Vanna shook the Drapers and Mr. Easton off as if they were drops of water after a shower. ". . . for tomorrow I shall do the same."

Vanna placed the tray on the ancient chopping block in the middle of the dungeon. "Eat, my little Gummi Bears. It's important for food to be well fed."

Vanna hadn't noticed that anything had changed

until she turned around. Then she filled the castle with a roar of pure rage. Laura Easton was gone. What Vanna had mistaken as hunger-driven enthusiasm on the part of her captives was really a trick. With Vanna's arms and legs full and her attention diverted, Laura had had little trouble slipping out the open dungeon door behind their captor. Then she ran.

Vanna was furious. Vanna was livid. Vanna was less than pleased. She quite literally stormed around the cell. Indoor lightning flashed and thunder rumbled as she flew around the walls and from floor to ceiling. The Drapers and Horace Easton held their ears, but Vanna's shrieks penetrated to the bone. She cursed. She howled. She swore. She grabbed Sammi by the collar and swiftly lifted him high off the floor.

Sammi could think of only one thing to say. "Can we eat now?"

Vanna was about to turn Sammi into a malted male shake on the spot when she heard a voice calling her from the kitchen. "Vanna, darling, did you lose this?"

Curley Red entered the dungeon carrying a furiously struggling Laura by the belt on her jeans. "I just love when I have to actually catch the food before I prepare it. It makes me feel all curdly inside."

Vanna smiled and gave Curley a quick kiss on his

totally shaved head. Her lips left bright red marks where they kissed. Laura looked at Vanna's mouth. She wasn't wearing any lipstick.

Vanna wagged her finger in front of Laura's face. "Bad food. Bad, bad food," she scolded.

Laura stuck out her tongue.

"Bad behavior often betters the broth." Curley stepped in and lashed out with the claws on his left hand.

Laura was just able to snap her tongue back into her mouth a millisecond before Curley's razor-sharp nails breezed by her lips.

"I prefer to work with hot-blooded foods." Curley checked his claws, found them empty, shrugged, and continued. "As I always tell my clients before they go shopping, the shorter the temper, the tastier the treat."

"Well." Vanna easily threw Laura over her shoulder and held on to her legs. "This hot tamale is heading for cold storage. My private pantry always seems to be the perfect punishment to make my food better-mannered."

With Laura kicking and screaming all the way, Vanna followed Curley out of the cell. Horace Easton tried to stop her, but a simple flick of one of Vanna's pinky fingers sent him sprawling head over heels across the dungeon floor.

"You don't have to worry about her for now." Vanna lifted Laura over her head with one hand. "I always save the best for last."

Laura quickly came to regret her escape attempt. If the dungeon was bad, Vanna's "private pantry" was much worse. It featured wall-to-wall cobwebs, and it smelled like the inside of an old sneaker that had been left out in a swamp.

"You can't leave me in here," Laura complained as Vanna dumped her onto a pile of empty burlap sacks in a corner. She choked on the dust that rose from the sacks and thought she felt a huge, hairy spider crawling down the back of her shirt.

"But it's the best room in the castle." Vanna sounded hurt. "I decorated it myself."

"Let me out!" Laura screamed while making a break for the door.

Vanna appeared in front of her, blocking her way. "You will stay here until it's time to be prepared."

"I don't wannnnaaaaa," Laura whined.

"Not another peep out of you, peachcakes, or else," Vanna ordered.

"Or else whaaaaaaaat?"

Vanna ran her tongue over her fangs. "Or else I'll have Curley whip up a little Laurazagna sauce right now."

Laura stopped whining, and Vanna left the pantry, locking the door behind her.

"Now, let's get down to business. What kind of dressing do you suggest?" Vanna asked Curley, who was floating back and forth across the kitchen outlining his plans for Vanna's party. "Are you going to serve them on a bed of weeds? Perhaps cactus collars? Blue suits are nice for almost any occasion."

Curley was renowned for dressing meals so beautifully that even the most controlled Vampire would have trouble waiting to bite in and chow down.

"Perhaps something different." Curley smiled. "Maybe we can make this a pajama dinner party."

"Eating food that's in pajamas? I love it!" Vanna clapped her hands. "It sounds so relaxing."

"Maybe everyone should wear pajamas." Curley giggled. "Guests included."

Vanna remembered the rip in her flannel sleeping cape and vetoed the idea. "For the food . . . fine. But I already told the guests it's black cape required."

"Very well." Curley was disappointed but moved on. "Now for the appetizers. Hmmm, let's see. Wait, I know." He raised a finger into the air. "How about some fresh Chips and dips."

"That would be delicious if you can find them," Vanna said.

"I've had my eye on a couple of dips, and maybe I can find some Chips in the phone book."

"You are a genius." Vanna shrieked with delight.

Vanna and Curley planned until almost dawn. The final decision involved dessert.

"Some frosted Laura drippings would be nice, but not too filling," Curley suggested. "Then there's always white-cell chocolate mousse or capillary pie."

Vanna had always had a sweet fang, so she ordered all three.

Vanna was absolutely exhausted when she finally snuggled down into her coffin. This promised to be her best party ever. The only thing that would really make it perfect would be for Vic to give up this teaching nonsense and join in the feeding frenzy. On that pleasant thought, Vanna closed her eyes and drifted off into a good day's sleep.

CHAPTER

Amanda, Gabe, Peter, Donny, and Amy all woke up early on Saturday morning. They all arrived at the school playground by 7:45 A.M. Nobody besides Donny brought anything. Teacher Vic had said he hoped to have everyone back home "before you know it" and that he'd supply everything they'd need for the rescue.

When Donny walked up to his friends, he was carrying a medium-sized brown paper bag.

"Teacher Vic said we weren't supposed to bring anything," Peter said, eyeing the bag. "What's in there?"

"In here?" Donny held the bag tightly. He looked around and whispered, "It's my Vampire Zapper."

"Cool!" Gabe said loudly. "Let's see."

"Shhh," Donny said as everybody gathered around. "Just a little peek."

Donny opened the bag, and everyone looked inside.

"A steak?" Amanda laughed. "You brought a steak?"

"Yep," Donny said. "A genuine New York strip. I got it out of our freezer this morning."

"I think you're a tad short on the concept," Amanda said, giggling. "Vampires are afraid of *s-t-a-k-e-s*, not *s-t-e-a-k-s*."

"Well, we just didn't happen to have an *s-t-a-k-e* in our freezer," Donny said sharply. "So I brought the next-best thing. I can pound this puppy right into any Vampire's heart." Donny felt the bag getting just a bit soggy. "As long as we get there before it thaws out."

"What a meathead." Amanda giggled. "No wonder you and Laura get along so well."

Amanda was still laughing at Donny when he offered her a piece of bubble gum. Without looking or thinking, Amanda unwrapped it and popped it into her mouth. As soon as she bit down, she knew she'd made a mistake. The taste of pure garlic filled her mouth, her nostrils, and the air around her. Amanda's cheeks puffed out, her eyes bulged, and the hair on the back of her neck stood at strict attention.

"I also got some of this garlic gum at the magic store." Donny smiled while Amanda spit out the gum and filled her mouth with half a container of Tic Tacs.

"Pretty neat, huh?" he asked. "I mean, for a meathead."

Before Amanda could finish chewing the Tic Tacs and respond, Amy changed the subject. "I wonder where Teacher Vic is." She looked at her watch. "He's late. It's already ten after eight."

"Wait a sec, maybe that's him." Gabe pointed to a figure that had just turned into the playground from the street. "At least I hope it's him, because if it's not him we're in trouble."

The solitary figure walked very slowly under the weight of a heavy black overcoat, which in turn covered a gray hooded sweatshirt. The hood was pulled up over a red ski mask and was tightened until only a hint of the mask and a very dark pair of sunglasses were visible. It had a dark brown blanket wrapped around its waist, which extended to its shoes. The shoes themselves were covered with black rubber boots. The figure held an open green-and-white golf umbrella over its head. To Amanda it looked more like a fashion designer's worst nightmare than a person.

"Uh-oh." Donny quickly dropped the bag with the steak into a trash can and stashed the gum in a pocket of his jeans. "It looks like whoever it is . . . is coming this way."

"It has to be Teacher Vic," Amy said.

"That's probably what Laura said before . . . you know." Donny's voice sounded shaky.

The figure had been moving very slowly, but by the time Donny said the word *you,* it was halfway across the playground. By the time he finished the word *know,* it was standing right next to him.

Before the five students could scream, the dark figure briefly lifted the sunglasses up over its eyes, separated the hood, and pulled its ski mask below its chin.

"Amy was right. It's me. What's up?" Teacher Vic's face was partially revealed, but only for a moment. Then the sunglasses, hood, and mask went back into place. "Sorry I'm late. Do you know that not a single store in this town carries sunscreen fifty-five hundred? They acted as if they never even heard of it. Anything below five thousand and I'd be bacon out here in about three minutes flat. Anyway, are you people ready to fly?"

Donny was surprised that Teacher Vic held only the umbrella in his hand. "I thought you were going to bring everything we needed."

"Oh, don't worry," Teacher Vic said. "To save

time in the V.K., I dropped stuff off at my parents' place last night. They're never home on weekends. I thought we'd stop there first and get changed."

"What are we going to change into?" Gabe said, half to himself.

"Where we're going, maybe you shouldn't ask," Amanda said as she chewed up the last of her Tic Tacs.

"Not to worry," Teacher Vic assured everyone. "I don't intend for any of you to become a pizza topping. I'll explain it all when we get there. We must be going." Teacher Vic looked up toward the cloudy sky. "That sun is a killer. Now, everyone grab hands and make a circle. It's all aboard the Vampire Express."

Teacher Vic kept the golf umbrella over his head by holding the hooked part of the handle between his teeth. He held Peter's hand on the right and Amy's on the left. He started to walk, pulling Peter and gently pushing against Amy's hand. Soon everyone in the circle was walking around and around. A moment later Teacher Vic quickened the pace.

Like a merry-go-round gone mad, the group moved faster and faster until all was a blur. Slowly the circle started to rise. Everyone's feet were moving so fast that at first no one realized that they were no longer touching the ground.

Peter was the first to notice that his Converse high-tops had lost touch with the concrete. He glanced down to see if his shoelaces were tied. They weren't, but it didn't matter. Peter knew there was absolutely no danger of stepping on them. What Peter saw was a pretty spectacular aerial view of the playground and the roof of the school—both of which were getting much smaller by the second.

Peter pulled on Amanda's hand and used his eyes to tell her to look down. By the time Amanda looked, she could see pretty much the whole city. An expression of shock came over her face, and Peter felt her grip tighten to the point of pain.

Then he pulled on Teacher Vic's hand and again used his eyes to tell Vic to look down. Teacher Vic just nodded rapidly and smiled a huge smile. Teacher Vic just loved to fly home, particularly when he could share the experience.

Meanwhile Amanda had signaled Gabe, who signaled Donny, who signaled Amy. Now all of them were looking down through the circle. Half the continent was visible, and the other half was quickly coming into view.

Everyone started to scream, but the wind was so strong that it seemed to blow the screams back into the screamers' mouths. No sounds were heard except for the sound of Teacher Vic's voice, which was as clear as if they were back in their classroom. "Hang on a little tighter. It's time to get this flight into high gear."

Within a quarter of a half of a second, everything the five students could recognize simply ceased to exist. What had been day became night, and then day again. The sun set in the east and the moon rose from the south. The stars had switched positions, and they were all different sizes and colors.

Amanda and Gabe thought they continued going up, while Peter, Amy, and Donny thought they were now going down. Still, the circle stayed intact.

Faster and faster they spun, until the circle appeared to be a solid ring of flannel and denim, freckles and flesh. The speed of light was a distant memory. The circle zoomed past sunbeams, and lightning looked as if it were traveling in slow motion. Then they landed with a bump.

"Where is this place?" Amy's voice quivered.

"*What* is this place?" Gabe's voice quaked.

"It—It sure ain't K-Kansas," Amanda stammered.

"It's home," Teacher Vic said happily. "Isn't it great?"

Great was not the word that immediately came to mind for any of Teacher Vic's traveling companions. The first word that popped into Amanda's head was *gloomy;* Gabe thought *grotesque;* Amy, *gruesome;*

Peter, *gross;* and the only word Donny kept thinking was *yuck*.

The place where the five students and one teacher had landed would have made the surface of the moon look like the Garden of Eden. Jagged gray rocks and short, leafless trees stretched out to three sides as far as the eye could see. At the horizon the land blended into the dark gray swirling clouds that filled the sky. Occasional bolts of lightning streaked from east to west, and a cold, clammy wind circled and embraced the travelers in a bone-chilling hug.

"Ahhh." Teacher Vic released Peter's and Amy's hands. "At least we have great weather." Teacher Vic motioned with his arm for everyone to follow him. "Come on, this way."

Teacher Vic led his students around a huge boulder that had blocked the view in that direction. When they made it past, Teacher Vic pointed and said, "There's the cottage. What do you think? I hope you like it."

Everyone looked where Teacher Vic pointed. There, looming before them, was Teacher Vic's parents' cottage. But this was certainly not like any cottage they'd ever seen before. The all-stone structure had three watchtowers and a moat. Its walls were each at least half a block long and three stories tall.

Peter couldn't stop staring at the carved gargoyle

that protruded out from above the main gate. It had the head of a hyena, the body of a lion, and the wings of a bat. "What's that?" Peter said, pointing.

Teacher Vic followed Peter's finger with his eyes. "Oh, that. I did that in arts and crafts at a night camp when I was five. Back then I always got my animals mixed up."

"I guess so," Peter said.

"I was only five," Teacher Vic said defensively. "How was I supposed to know that it should have been a wolf's head? Back then I had a thing for hyenas. Even my best friend was a hyena."

"I liked guppies," Peter said softly.

"To each his own," Teacher Vic said. "Come on, let's get inside. This daylight traveling is really tiring me out."

Teacher Vic pulled a garage-door opener out of his cape. When he pushed the button, a drawbridge lowered over the moat and the group walked into the "cottage."

Once inside, the students expected to see suits of armor, swords, and shields, or at the very least the ghosts of dinners past. Instead the group walked into a very nicely decorated living room with an overstuffed chair and an early-American plaid sofa bed with matching hassock.

"Look at this." Peter ran over to a huge-screen TV complete with VCR and cable box.

"And this." Amy was checking out a CD system that looked as if it could really rock the castle.

Teacher Vic dragged a trunk out from behind the aquarium. "You people are going to look just great." He opened the trunk and handed out neatly folded black shirts, carefully pressed black pants, and outstanding black velvet capes with satin linings. He also gave each a perfectly fitting pair of black patent leather shoes.

"Why the costumes?" Donny asked.

"Back in the human realm these indeed would be costumes," Vic said. "But here a flannel shirt or a T-shirt and blue jeans are considered to be appropriate only on Halloween, or to scare the death out of your parents. Remember, Donny, this is the Vampire Kingdom. It is extremely important that you dress accordingly."

Teacher Vic returned to the trunk. "You also might need these." He pulled out five small glass boxes. Each contained two white pointy things.

Donny looked at Gabe, who shrugged an *I have no idea what they are* shrug.

The mystery was solved when Teacher Vic held out his hands and said proudly, "Here're your fangs."

"Fangs?" Amy sounded about one snaky lick away from being totally grossed out.

"Not real fangs," Vic said. "Just caps for your canines. My cousin, Vern, is a dentist."

"They're so cool." Peter had already slipped his fangs in place and tried to bite Amanda on the neck. He failed when she punched him in the nose.

"Be careful. Those fangs are not toys. They're very expensive," Teacher Vic warned. "Vern's fangs are the best in the V.K. They've kept many a toothless Vampire from starving or having to use a straw."

Teacher Vic once again stuck his head into the trunk. "Just put the Vampire-wear on over your other clothing. The V.K. tends to leave humans cold."

"Why do we have to dress up in this stuff?" Gabe moaned, sounding just a bit frightened. "Can't we just go get Laura and get out?"

"That is exactly what I hope will happen, Gabriel." Teacher Vic continued searching through the trunk. "But what if we run into a Vampire with insomnia?"

Teacher Vic retrieved a brown paper bag from the bottom of the trunk. "Or what if we're delayed?" Teacher Vic stared at Gabe, who felt a chill travel up one arm and down the other. "What if it gets dark,

Gabriel? Do you want to be strolling around here in your blue jeans and Raiders T-shirt . . . after dark?"

"I gotta be home for dinner." Gabe quickly started putting on the black pants over his jeans. "And we eat early."

Teacher Vic quickly spilled the contents of the paper bag onto his parents' coffee table. Five tubes of white greasepaint makeup and five aerosol cans with labels reading LARD-NET EXTRA HOLD HAIR SPRAY rolled across the wood.

"You're not, like, serious?" Amanda twisted a lock of her curly hair around a finger.

"Like, totally serious." Teacher Vic thought he sounded just like Amanda. Amanda thought he just sounded like a dork.

"All of the young Vampires are into the slicked-back look," Teacher Vic continued. "If anyone sees us, we don't want to attract a lot of attention."

"And this white glop?" Peter had unscrewed the top and was enjoying the smell of the greasepaint.

"Your skin," Teacher Vic said. "It's so rosy and tan. You look really unhealthy, for Vampires."

"We're not Vampires," Gabe said.

"Until we free Vanna's dinner, that's exactly what you must appear to be."

About fifteen minutes later each of the five sixth-graders looked as if he or she had just gotten out of a coffin.

"Beautiful." Teacher Vic brushed away a tear. "You all look so beautiful." Then he sniffed the air. "But . . ."

"But what?" Donny looked into a makeup mirror and almost gave himself a heart attack. He was a flesh-and-blood human inside, but outside he was covered with a hard Vampire shell.

"You all look as if you could be my relatives," Teacher Vic said, "but you smell so . . . so appetizingly human. If we don't do something, your scent will have Vampires waking up all along the way between here and Vanna's thinking that breakfast is being served."

Teacher Vic reached into the trunk and found a big spray bottle filled with a murky brown liquid. He immediately turned and started spraying.

The kids tried to spin away fast, but the spray was much faster. *Yuck*'s, *ick*'s, and yowls of disgust filled the room as each student was coated from head to toe. The five held their noses and coughed. Teacher Vic breathed in deeply and sighed a happy sigh.

"What's in this stuff?" Peter choked out the question.

"Just some bat sweat, slug oil, and grave droppings. The scent is very *in* this year." Teacher Vic shook the bottle. "Plus, properly shaken, not stirred, it's really quite delicious."

Gabe almost threw up when Teacher Vic offered him a swig. "No?" Teacher Vic put the bottle back into the trunk. "Maybe later."

"Oh boy, do I stink," Donny said.

"We all stink." Peter pinched his nose.

"Aren't you going to say something about your sister stinking?" Amy asked, fully expecting Peter to take advantage of the opportunity.

"Nah," Peter said. "Even she doesn't smell this bad . . . usually."

Teacher Vic couldn't be more pleased. "Now not only do you look like Vampires, you smell like them, too."

"Haven't you guys in the V.K. ever heard of deodorant?" Peter asked.

"What's that?"

"Thought so."

"I think it's time we do what we came here to do." Teacher Vic looked proudly at his students. "Ready, everyone—let's rescue!" Teacher Vic cheered and reached into the trunk. He pulled out the new cape his parents had given him and threw it around his shoulders. Amy noticed that it still had a price tag on it from a store named Capers. The tag read: 6 PINTS, A NEG.

"Where to now?" Amanda asked.

"Vanna's castle . . . nonstop."

"How are we going to get there? Fly?"

"Nah." Teacher Vic started walking out of the living room. He motioned for everyone to follow. "Let's take the Jeep."

CHAPTER

As Vanna slept and Laura paced the pantry, Teacher Vic and his students were on their way. Teacher Vic had decided to take his parents' Jeep for two reasons. One, in the Vampire Kingdom there's less chance of being spotted on the ground than in the air, and two, he just liked to drive.

Everyone except Teacher Vic was almost hypnotized by the bleak, barren landscape through which they drove. The view was made even drearier by the fact that the Jeep's windows were tinted nearly black —a very popular option in the V.K.

It was so dark in the Jeep that the students could barely see the person next to them, but they could look out at a scene that featured absolutely no signs of life. The ground was cracked, gray, and without even a single blade of grass. What trees there were looked gnarled and leafless.

"I thought you said we were going to take the scenic route to Vanna's castle," Amy said.

"Yeah," Vic answered happily. "Do you like it?"

Donny shivered as he watched a new, deep crack appear in the ground just off the road. "Teacher Vic." Donny's voice shook. "Can we fly the rest of the way? It would save a lot of time."

"We have plenty of time," Teacher Vic assured him. "Just relax and enjoy the view."

"You know," Peter said to the teacher, "Donny might be right." He looked out the driver's-side window. "It does seem to be getting a little darker out there. I think maybe we should hurry up."

"Don't worry." Teacher Vic looked at his watch. "It's only three forty-five. There's lots of light left."

As he continued to drive, Teacher Vic believed every word he said. Unfortunately, in all of his planning he'd forgotten one little detail—the time difference between the human world and the V.K. The V.K. is always exactly three hours and seventeen minutes ahead of human time.

Teacher Vic didn't know it as he drove along humming the theme from *The Addams Family,* but Peter was right, it was getting late. Very, very late.

Laura hadn't slept a wink all day. She had felt every inch of the pantry wall, searching for a way out.

Now that the day was almost over, she began searching for a place to hide.

According to Teacher Vic's watch, the Jeep slowly pulled into Vanna's castle's driveway at about four o'clock in the afternoon. But when they stepped out onto the driveway, he noticed that it was already starting to get dark.

"I don't get it." Teacher Vic tapped on his watch. "We should still have almost four hours before breakfast."

"Uh, does that tell you anything?" Peter pointed to a clock embedded in the stone above Vanna's drawbridge. It read 7:17.

"Nuts," Teacher Vic said, tossing his watch into the moat. "I forgot all about nightdark saving time. On second thought, Peter . . . I think we'd *better* hurry it up."

Teacher Vic knew that they had only about a half hour to do the deed and depart on schedule. Fortunately he also knew that Vanna always hid a spare key to the drawbridge under the unwelcome mat in case she ever locked herself out. With little time lost, the rescuers were in the castle and on their way to save the day.

As they snuck through the shadowy corridors, Teacher Vic peeked into Vanna's burial room to make sure she was still asleep. Sure enough, her coffin was closed up tight. The TV was on and was blaring out a blood-supplement infomercial that claimed to be able to make anyone fly higher, bite deeper, and suck necks harder.

Vanna had once told Vic that she loved falling asleep with the TV on. She had been one of the first in the entire V.K. to get cable. After that she was hooked on the all-infomercial station.

Many Vampires secretly laughed at Vanna's taste in TV programming, but no one dared to bare a single fang in her presence. While Vanna was one of the most beautiful Vampires, she was also one of the most powerful, nasty, and respected.

Only Vic's sister, Vivian, was considered to have comparable powers, but she'd never been tested. Vivian didn't like to show off, and anyway, since she was several centuries younger, Vivian always let Vanna be the center of attention whenever she flew into the room.

Teacher Vic remembered that Vanna always kept her food in the dungeon, just off the kitchen. The rescuers hurried down one hall, past the Jacuzzi, by the living room, through the dining room, and into the kitchen. Teacher Vic pointed to a huge metal door between the microwave and the broom closet.

"They're in there." He noticed the ever-darkening sky through the window above the sink. "Let's get them, and let's fly."

No one argued with their teacher's suggestion. Teacher Vic wasn't the only one who'd looked at the sky. Amanda grabbed the huge key that hung from a rusty hook next to the door and fit it into the lock. It took all her strength, but she managed to turn it and push open the dungeon door.

"We're going to make it." Teacher Vic giggled. "I can't believe it, but we're going to make it."

Teacher Vic and the five students raced into the cell. Horace Easton and the Drapers greeted them by jumping up and down and cheering. The jumping stopped when Horace put his hands over the Drapers' mouths and, remembering what they had tried to do to Teacher Vic, asked, "You are here to *rescue* us, aren't you?"

Teacher Vic couldn't resist having just a bit of fun. He bared his fangs, flared his nostrils, floated toward the now terrified trio, and finally said, "Sure. Why not?"

The Drapers resumed jumping, and Horace patted Teacher Vic on the back. "I really, *really* hate to admit this, but you know, for a teacher, you're not half bad."

Teacher Vic smiled graciously and accepted the half compliment while looking around the dungeon for Laura. All the students were doing the same.

"Where's Laura?" Teacher Vic whispered.

"Oh, she tried to escape," Horace Easton said with a huge smile.

"She what?" Teacher Vic shouted with an equally impressive frown.

"Shhh," Peter, Amanda, Amy, Gabe, and Donny all said as they nervously looked back out at Vanna's kitchen to see if anyone was coming.

"She what?" Teacher Vic whispered a whisper that sounded like a shout.

Horace Easton snapped his suspenders and said proudly, "She tried to escape."

"And what happened?" Donny asked.

"Oh, some guy named Burley Bed or something caught her and brought her back."

"You mean Curley Red, the caterer?" Vic moaned.

"Yeah, that's the guy." Horace was still smiling. "But don't worry. As Vanna was taking her away, she said she was going to save her for last. All we have to do is go get her, and get out of—"

"This is horrible!" Teacher Vic cried, and floated up from the floor, his cape rustling around him. "How could Laura do something so . . . so

74

wrong?" Vic let loose with a most savage howl to release his tension.

Mr. Easton ran and hid behind the Drapers.

"Shhhhhh!" the five students insisted, sure that the howl was loud enough to wake the dead. "Get ahold of yourself, Teacher Vic."

Teacher Vic was not about to be shushed. He flew into a fit. "If Vanna didn't drain Laura on the spot for trying to escape, it means she's put her in her private pantry."

"So," Sammi Draper said. "Go get her out, why don'tcha?"

Teacher Vic grabbed Sammi by the shoulders. "I don't feel you realize the peril Laura's escape puts all of us in."

"Whew, well, that's a relief," Sammi said happily as Teacher Vic released his grip. "I thought you were going to say that we were all in some kind of danger or something."

"What do you think *peril* means, Mr. Stupid?" Sam asked his brother.

"I know what it is," Sammi said. "And I'm not stupid."

"Okay," Sam said. "What is it?"

Sammi cleared his throat and held up one finger. "A *peril* is a little round white jewelry thingy that you get out of those weird shell thingies in the sea."

"Wrong, oyster breath. *Peril* means *danger*," Sam said angrily.

Sammi scratched his chin. "Perils are dangerous? Then I really don't think we should have bought Mom that necklace, no matter how good a deal that guy in the bus-station bathroom said it was."

Sam groaned as Sammi continued. "But anyway, what does our mom's necklace have to do with Laura and us?"

"Yeah," Horace Easton agreed. "You know where Laura is, so get us out of here and then go get her."

"The fact that Laura is gone is precisely why you have to remain here. There's only one key to Vanna's private pantry, and Vanna keeps that on a little chain around her neck. Until we get that key, no one can be allowed to suspect that anything is amiss with the meal. You must stay here." Teacher Vic looked out at the sky. Sunset in twelve minutes and counting.

The Drapers and Horace Easton made a break for the door. "If we stay here, we're horseradish."

"And if you don't, Laura's goose is cooked." Teacher Vic made eye contact with Sam, who was in the lead. Sam froze in his tracks, causing Sammi to run into him and freeze as well. Horace, who was bringing up the rear, ran into Sammi and also became part of the ice sculpture. They looked like the Three Stooges playing statues.

"Come on, gang." Teacher Vic started walking out of the dungeon. "We only have about ten minutes before Vanna awakens. We have to get the key off her, find Laura, and get out of here before that happens."

"Do we still have time?" Amanda asked.

"I think so."

Teacher Vic didn't know it, but their time was just about to run out. He hadn't taken one full step out of the dungeon when a very familiar voice said, "Vic, darling! I thought I heard you."

Vanna flew to Vic and threw her arms around him. "I knew you'd come, I just knew it. Underneath you're all Vampire."

While he was being hugged, Vic motioned behind his back for everyone to hide in the cell.

Vanna playfully nipped Vic's neck. "But my, aren't you the naughty one? Sneaking into the cell for an hors d'oeuvre, are we?"

Vic laughed and played along. "Guilty as charged." He threw up his hands. Then he gestured with his head toward the Drapers and Horace. "But I'm afraid I had to freeze them before I could sneak a taste. They tried to run."

Vanna glanced into the cell without actually entering it. After seeing the three people frozen together, she accepted Vic's explanation. "No matter," she said happily. "They'll keep better that way."

Vanna took one sniff of the cell air, and, smelling nothing human other than the three entrees, she pulled Vic all the way into the kitchen and closed the dungeon door.

Since the Drapers and Laura's dad were in no condition to travel, Vanna didn't bother to lock the door, a fact that did not go unnoticed by Teacher Vic or the students hiding in the cell.

"By the way, Van, where's Laura?" Teacher Vic moved toward a door that led out of the kitchen. Vanna followed.

"Why do you ask?"

"Oh"—Vic thought fast—"because she promises to be the tastiest of the bunch, and I wanted to make sure that you didn't have one of your special brunches without inviting me."

"Of course not, darling," Vanna cooed. "She's in my private pantry." Vanna played with the key on the chain around her neck. "The little juice box actually tried to *escape*."

"Escape?" Teacher Vic laughed. "From you?"

"I know." Vanna placed her hand on Vic's shoulder. "The nerve of some food."

"Oh well." Teacher Vic smiled. "I'm sure she'll taste better than she acts."

"That's my Victor!" Vanna held Vic's arm. "I am so wickedly delighted that you're here. I was afraid you wouldn't come."

"Could anyone ever say no to you?" Vic asked.

"No." Vanna squeezed Vic's arm a bit too tightly. "Remember that."

Vic and Vanna stared into each other's eyes for several seconds before they started to laugh. With Vic in the lead, they laughed their way through the door and out of the kitchen.

In the dungeon Peter, Amy, Donny, Amanda, and Gabe had pressed themselves flat against the same wall that the door was on. Had Vanna walked into the cell, she would have seen them as soon as she turned to leave. But Vanna saw no reason to enter once she'd noticed that her dinners were frozen and had sniffed the air. Teacher Vic's Vampire spray had worked, and his students were most grateful.

"I think I'm starting to love to stink," Peter said. They all moved away from the wall as soon as they could no longer hear Teacher Vic's and Vanna's laughter.

"I don't think I'll take a shower for a year," Donny said.

"So, what else is new?" Amanda teased.

"Hey, I take showers," Donny said defensively.

Peter changed the subject. "We have to find Laura. You heard Vanna. Teacher Vic was right, Laura's in her pantry. Let's find it and wait for Teacher Vic to get there with the key."

"But how are we going to find the pantry?" Donny whined. "We don't know where it is and we only have a few minutes before dark."

"Then we'd better look fast." Peter pulled open the dungeon door and led everyone out to begin the search.

Unfortunately for Peter and the rest, they didn't search quite fast enough. The students didn't even come close to finding Laura before shadows grew long and the sun set.

Meanwhile, in the pantry, Laura started to tremble with fear. She hid under the burlap sacks, knowing full well that Vanna would have no trouble finding her. Although the pantry had no window, there was a tiny crack in the wall near the ceiling. All day long a single streak of sunlight had been able to shine through. Now it was gone.

No sooner had her last ray of hope vanished than Laura heard the doorbell ring.

———

Gabe, Amy, Donny, Peter, and Amanda were just passing the front door when the sun officially set. Thousands of candles started to light mysteriously all around the castle, and the doorbell rang.

Everyone practically jumped out of their cape in panic. "What do we do now?" Gabe asked as the doorbell rang again, again, and again.

Peter looked at his friends in their outfits, fang caps, and makeup. The doorbell kept ringing. "I think we should answer the door."

Before anyone could say "Are you a total loon, or what?" Peter threw open the door and found himself standing face-to-face with Curley Red and his sister, Venessa, who had come along to help.

"Good evening," Peter said in a deep voice while trying to stop his knees from shaking. "Welcome to Vanna's castle. My name is . . ." Peter paused. "My name is Veter. We are all here to assist you."

"Look, Curley," the female Vampire said. "How adorably cute. Vanna must have hired a troop of Vampire Scouts as waiters for the evening. That Vamp is so civic-minded."

"Odd." Curley Red scratched his chin. "Vanna said nothing about waiters."

"Vanna wanted us to help you in any way we can," Amanda jumped in before Curley could do any more thinking. She remembered the name Teacher Vic had

81

mentioned in the cell. "How can we serve you, O Curley Red the Great?" She bowed her head.

"You've heard of me?"

It was quite obvious that Curley liked what Amanda had to say.

"Curley Red the Magnificent," Peter continued the compliment parade.

"What can I say besides 'correct'?"

"Curley Red the Exalted." Amy bowed.

"What intelligent Scouts."

"The Glorious." Gabe bowed.

"Stop, you're embarrassing me." Curley looked at Donny. "Well?"

"Curley Red the . . . the . . ." Donny was having a bit of trouble. "The Totally Cool."

" 'Totally Cool'?" Curley and Venessa said simultaneously.

"A human term." Amanda again came to the rescue. "It means that you're better than the best could possibly ever be."

"Yes, I see. Good. Good!" Curley nodded. "If you're going to help me prepare the food, I'm pleased that you can speak its language."

"Thank you, Your Most Major Dorkiness." Peter smiled from below his bow.

Amanda shot Peter a terrified look, afraid that he might have blown everything.

82

"Another human term?" Curley smiled.

"Oh yes," Peter said. "And it fits you so perfectly."

"Thank you." Curley blushed.

"Maybe we should just call you Dork for short," Amanda suggested, feeling quite relieved.

"Oh, you honor me too much." Curley blushed some more. "But please . . . in public make it Mr. Dork."

"Yes, sir, Mr. Dork." Amanda saluted.

"And what's your name, dear?" Curley asked Amanda pleasantly.

"Ah, ah, ah, Vamanda?"

"I have a niece named Vamanda."

"Hum," Curley's sister hummed as she started to examine Gabe's cape. "Hum-hum-hum."

"What's wrong, Venessa?" Curley asked.

"Nothing really. But now that I can get a closer look, I have to say that I've never seen Scout capes like these before. There are no rankings, troop numbers, or demerit badges."

"We're off-duty?" Gabe offered an explanation.

"Yeah." Amy stepped in front of Gabe. "And we're all from different troops. Vanna didn't want to play favorites."

"Vanna might be vicious." Curley Red looked at Venessa and nodded. "But she is fair."

"True," Venessa agreed. "But what level of Scouts are you?"

"We're Vulture Scouts," Peter blurted out. He instantly regretted the blurt. *You idiot,* Peter thought. *Who ever heard of Vulture Scouts?*

The two Vampires looked at each other, then slowly back at the students. Peter was about to try to talk his way out of the trouble he assumed he had talked them into when Venessa said, "Vulture Scouts? That is marvelous. I never made it past Leech."

"Come, Venessa," Curley said. "We must get to work."

As he passed Peter, Curley leaned down and whispered into his ear, "She really never made it past Mosquito."

When Curley Red and Venessa floated out of the room, the students breathed a collective sigh of relief. That feeling lasted only about three seconds.

Curley stuck his head back into the room and shouted, "Well, what are you Scouts waiting for? Unload the truck."

Over the next hour the human Vampire look-alikes unloaded a huge assortment of peculiar parcels, packages, and platters from a large black truck. The words CURLEY RED'S BLOOD VESSELS were painted in scarlet letters on each door. Curley had let the paint drip down the door so that it looked as if the words were bleeding. His blood "vessels" were considered the most tasteful and tantalizing catering trucks in the V.K.

Peter and Donny brought in large barrels marked DIP MIX and CHIP MIX. They had no idea what Curley Red meant when he said, "I hope Vanna isn't too disappointed that I couldn't find fresh."

While Curley and Venessa placed arrangements of wilted black roses and weeds on Vanna's seventy-foot-long black marble dining room table, Amanda and Amy carried in four huge sterling silver serving platters. The platter covers were so large that they looked like shiny domed tents.

"I hope this isn't what it sounds like." Gabe grimaced, plopping down a box marked CREAM OF PIGEON PASTA and another labeled HAMSTER HELPER onto the kitchen counter.

Before they were through, the five students had lugged in vats of blood pudding, crates of corpuscle quiche, and gallons of globulin *au gratin*. Finally, when Amanda carried in four pairs of black pajamas with stars on the tops and full moons on the bottoms, the truck was empty.

"Now what can we do, Mr. Dork?" Peter asked Curley, who had just finished stringing black streamers across the dining room.

"Answer the door," Curley said a moment before the doorbell rang. "Greet the guests while Venessa and I dress the meal."

Vanna and Teacher Vic returned from the short flight they had taken around the neighborhood just as the first guest arrived. The key to the pantry still hung loosely on the chain around Vanna's neck. Teacher Vic had waited for an opportunity to get it, but that opportunity had not knocked.

When Vanna heard about the Vampire Scouts, she almost flew into a rage of suspicion. Teacher Vic calmed her somewhat by saying that he had arranged for the Scouts as a surprise for Vanna.

This time Vanna's nip on Teacher Vic's neck was less playful. "I hate surprises," she snarled softly. "Don't ever do it again."

By the time the last guests had arrived, the sixth-graders were exhausted but as delighted as they could possibly be on "student night" at a Vampire's castle. The Vampires were mingling throughout Vanna's three-story living room. With feasting on their minds and grumbling in their stomachs, they were focusing on the upcoming meal. So far no one suspected a thing.

CHAPTER

Teacher Vic was starting to get desperate. He floated around the living room, forcing himself to make small talk with Vampires and looking for a chance to get the key from Vanna. He knew he'd have to make his move quickly. These were hungry Vampires, and they were getting hungrier by the second.

The Vampire guests were not making Teacher Vic's job any easier. Wherever he flew, someone would stop him and ask why he'd ever started to like humans and how he'd been able to break free of the disgusting habit. Until he found a way to grab that key and free Laura, the partygoers had to be convinced that Vic was once again the mean, cruel, savage, wicked, and downright naughty Vampire they had always known and loved.

"So what made you come to your senses?" Vic's old accountant and pal, Vlad, asked.

"Yes," Virginia said, floating into the conversation. "We were all so horribly worried about you when you decided to become a . . . become a . . . teacher of . . ."

"Say it, Virginia." Vlad patted her on the back. "It's okay. We're all Vampires here."

"of . . . humans." Virginia closed her eyes and lowered her head in shame.

Vic smiled broadly and shrugged. "Hey, we all make mistakes. I should have known that once you're a Vampire, it's in the blood."

Virginia and several others were about to question him further when Vanna strolled up and put her cape around Vic's shoulders. Vic considered himself Vanna's *ex*-boyfriend. Vanna had never accepted the "ex" part. She thought Vic's decision to come to her dinner proved that he still loved her, and she wasn't about to waste any time on formalities.

"Isn't it wonderful that Vic and I are back together?" Vanna giggled a giggle that was more like a growl. "I thought I had lost him forever. And now . . ." Vanna paused and giggle-grrred some more. "Now we're engaged."

"Why, you little demonoid." Virginia winked at Vic. "Why didn't you tell us the news?"

Vic hadn't told them because Vanna's announcement was news to him. Vic just smiled and said nothing while Vanna gave him a hug that would have crushed a Volkswagen.

When she finally released him, Vic whispered in Vanna's ear, "Engaged?"

"I knew you'd agree," Vanna whispered back. "Isn't it wonderful how everything is working out so well?"

Things were not working out quite so well for Curley Red in the kitchen. He and Venessa were desperately trying to get the Drapers and Horace Easton dressed for dinner in the black pajamas, but they were having a devil of a time doing it.

"Frozen food!" Curley huffed. "How do they expect us to properly prepare frozen food? Sure, by first puncture they'll be all thawed out and mushy, but does anyone think of the caterer? I think not."

Curley managed to get Sammi's right arm through a pajama sleeve, but when he did, the left arm popped out and punched him in the stomach.

"Can we help you?" Amanda asked, trying not to laugh.

"No!" Curley pushed Sammi's left arm into a pajama sleeve, causing his right arm to spring free and smack him in the ear. "This is a job for professionals only. It takes a delicate touch to bend the flesh but not to break it. Do not try this at home."

"Don't worry, we won't." Peter turned away and coughed to cover his laughter.

"Why don't you Scouts serve the hors d'oeuvres?" Venessa said while trying to get a pair of pajama bottoms onto Horace's legs, which were frozen in a running position. "We prepared the trays while you were greeting the guests."

Venessa tumbled to the dungeon floor, and Horace toppled on top of her. "They're in the refrigerator, bottom shelves," she said impatiently.

Amanda, Peter, Gabe, Amy, and Donny each grabbed a different tray or bowl and removed its foil covering.

"Oh, gross!" Amy almost passed out when she got one whiff of what was under the foil.

"Thank you." Curley blushed. "My mucous mushroom caps are always a favorite."

Amy vowed silently never to eat again.

Peter's and Donny's trays each held a dozen rows of crackers. Every cracker had a clump of red, sticky, stringy things spread on it. Peter's was the worst. The red, sticky, stringy things on his tray were still moving.

Gabe held an ashen-gray soup tureen that contained a steaming red broth. A small label on the bowl identified it as Curley's Famous Cream of Cadaver Soup.

And Amanda held a tray of nachos, which looked okay, until Venessa reminded her that nachos à la A negative were best slurped at body temperature.

"Don't just stand there admiring the food!" Curley scolded the Scouts from inside the dungeon. "Serve it."

Curley had somehow managed to get both his head and Sammi's through the pajama top's neck opening. "And remember . . . no nibbling!"

"No problem." Peter looked down as the red strands of stinky goo wiggled off the crackers and slithered around his tray. "We're not that hungry."

Everyone tried to breathe only through their mouth and not look down as they went out to serve Vanna's dinner guests. As soon as they entered the living room, the students were pounced upon by snarling, snapping Vampires. A minute or so later all the hors d'oeuvres were gone. Peter's was the most popular tray. The stringy glop was the first to go.

"Yum." Vanna licked her lips after the feeding frenzy was over. "Curley's outdone himself this time."

Curley Red's hors d'oeuvres were one of Vic's favorite treats. But he didn't even take a taste for fear of frightening his students.

"Why aren't you eating?" Vanna asked.

"I'm saving room for some warm Laura and a nice

chilled Draper." Vic smiled. "In fact it really is getting a little late. Why don't I help Curley thaw out the dungeon delights? Or . . . I know." Teacher Vic snapped his fingers. "I'll go get Laura out of the pantry. That will really save Curley a lot of time."

Teacher Vic reached for the chain around Vanna's neck, which held the key to the success of the rescue mission. She slapped his hand away. "Patience, my darling. I don't want her to have any pints missing before she's served to our guests. It just wouldn't look good. Besides, even a little slurp now would spoil your dinner."

"I was only trying to help." Vic couldn't take his eyes off the key.

"To help yourself, you mean." Vanna laughed. "You can't fool me, Victor. You never could."

Teacher Vic did his best to hide his bitter disappointment. It was rapidly approaching midnight . . . the dinner hour. This had been his best chance to get the pantry key and free Laura. Now it looked as if his chances had zoomed past slim and were rapidly approaching none.

"And besides," Vanna continued, "you hired the Scouts, let them do the work."

In one swift movement Vanna unfastened her necklace, slid off the key, and tossed it to Peter. "Here, pup, earn your pay."

Teacher Vic's mood took a quick swing for the better. He smiled broadly. "Vanna," he said slowly, "you are beautiful."

"Tell me about it." Vanna fluffed her hair.

When Vic didn't say anything right away, she snarled and pulled him into a corner of the room. "I said . . . tell me about it!"

CHAPTER

"Look what I have." Peter happily dangled the large golden key in front of him as he burst through the door to the kitchen. "Vanna just gave it to me. Can you believe it? She just gave it to me."

"And now you will give it to me. Thank you for saving me a trip." Curley Red snatched the key out of Peter's hand.

Teacher Vic appeared through the parlor door behind Curley. He reached over the caterer's shoulder and plucked the key away before Curley could react. "And now *you* will give it to *me*."

"*How dare . . .*" Curley turned, prepared to give the key-grabber a clawing he'd never forget. His plans changed when he saw who that grabber was. Curley had heard the news of Vanna and Vic's engagement and he hoped to cater what promised to be the Vampire wedding of the eternity.

"What were you going to say?" Teacher Vic raised

an eyebrow and swung the key around in circles on his pinky finger.

"Ummm—Ahh—Ummm," Curley stammered.

"Yes?" Teacher Vic raised his other eyebrow and stopped swinging the key.

"I was saying, Howdy. *Dare* I say what a magnificent cape you're wearing?" Curley spoke fast. "It's from Capers, no?"

Teacher Vic nodded while Curley kept talking. "May I congratulate you on your engagement? You and Vanna will make such a terrifyingly malevolent couple."

"Thank you," Vic said politely.

"I mean it sincerely." Curley straightened the collar on Vic's cape. "Oh, I don't know if you're aware of the fact that I also do weddings."

"Your engagement?" Amanda and the rest of the students had joined in the conversation.

"It's a long story." Vic rolled his eyes just the way he'd seen Amanda do it in class. The expression looked pretty geeky on a Vampire.

"I'd stick to sneering." Amanda patted him on the arm. "It's more you."

"Weddings, holidays, death days, but I'm particularly proud of my weddings. You know I did the Princess Die affair." Curley continued his sales pitch. "As we always say, 'For something gooey and deliciously bloody . . . call Curley Red, your neck-suckin' buddy.' "

"I think he should say, 'He's like a dirty devil with a big pitchfork. If that's cool with you, call Mr. Dork,' " Peter whispered to Gabe.

"Thank you." Curley had overheard the comment, and he shook Peter's hand. "Mind if I use that?"

"Not at all, O Great Dorkest of Dorkey Dorks." Peter bowed. "In fact, I wish you would."

"Boy, I like that lad." Curley winked at Teacher Vic. "He'll make a great caterer one day."

Suddenly there was a loud clattering like metal wheels on cobblestones. Everyone looked to see Curley's sister, Venessa, pushing three serving carts, one lined up behind the other like railroad boxcars, out of the dungeon. Each cart held a huge, sparkling sterling silver serving tray with an enormous domed lid.

"Speaking of great caterers . . ." Venessa pushed the carts forward until the lead cart ran into the back of her brother's knees, causing them to buckle forward. "The first three courses are ready to be served."

Curley straightened out his knees and glared at his sister. "How many times have you done that to me?"

"Six thousand three hundred and seventy-seven."
Venessa gave the carts another slight push. "I mean
six thousand three hundred and seventy-eight."

"Wait till I tell Mom." Curley again straightened
out his knees. This time he moved away from the
carts before the count continued to rise.

Curley walked to the side of the first cart and lifted
the lid off the platter. There a still semifrozen Horace
Easton was scrunched down on his elbows and
knees. His moon-covered bottom stuck up in the air,
and you could see the reflection of his bloodred face
on the sparkling silver tray. Horace's neck was
shaved, washed, polished, and accented with sprigs
of brown, dead parsley. A large rotten apple had
been stuck into his mouth.

"Gorgeous! Absolutely gorgeous!" Curley clapped
his hands. "The appearance of food is so important,
don't you think? I always say, if it looks good, it'll
taste better."

Being extracareful not to make a cut with his fin-
gernail, Curley ran a finger over Horace Easton's
neck. He then licked it, thought about it, and
smacked his lips. "Needs a little salt. Venessa, dear,
would you mind?"

"Always more salt," Venessa complained as she
headed back to the dungeon, where she'd left the

shaker. "No matter how much I sprinkle, it's always more salt and more—"

"Neck tenderizer, dear." Curley licked his finger again and called after his sister. "I don't think you used quite enough neck tenderizer."

As soon as Venessa disappeared through the dungeon door, Teacher Vic quickly moved to Peter and whispered something into his ear. Peter nodded, smiled, and followed in Venessa's footsteps.

"Wait, Venessa," Peter said as he approached the dungeon. "Let me help you. Curley Red should not be made to wait."

"I really like that lad." Curley smiled. "Maybe I'll let him puncture a minor artery before serving the food."

Venessa's opinion of Peter was less positive than her brother's. "I already have them, you little kiss-up," Venessa called to Peter as she was returning from the far side of the dungeon with the salt and neck tenderizer. "Talk about trying to be the caterer's pet, you brussels sprouts lov—"

Nobody heard Venessa say the *er* in *lover*. Peter had beaten her to the cell door and closed it tight. He quickly grabbed the key from next to the door and locked it before a shocked Venessa had time to react.

Vanna's dungeon had appeared in *Dungeon Beau-*

tiful magazine a month before and was the envy of every Vampire in the V.K. It was designed so that even a Vampire could be held captive for a short period.

At the muffled sound of Venessa's fists pounding on the dungeon door and her barely audible screams of rage, Curley Red started to laugh. "That will teach you to use enough neck tenderizer." He patted Peter on the back.

After several more minutes of laughing and pointing at his sister's furious face through the slat in the dungeon door, Curley turned to Peter. "Great joke, lad. But I'm afraid it's time to let her out. You have a first course to serve, and we have a Laura to prepare."

Peter threw the dungeon key to Teacher Vic, who caught it in the same hand that held the key to Vanna's private pantry.

"I don't think so." Teacher Vic shook his head.

"What's going on here?" Curley looked from Teacher Vic to Peter.

After getting a nod from his teacher, Peter smiled and removed his fangs. Gabe, Amanda, Amy, and Donny did the same.

"You're food!" Curley shrieked as he raced for the door that led to the dining room. "Food on the loose! Food on the loose!" he yelled, trying to sound the warning.

Teacher Vic suddenly blocked Curley's path. He stared into Curley's eyes. "I think it's time for the caterer to become the catered."

What's taking him so long? Vanna strummed her nails on the dining room table and impatiently tapped her foot on the floor. It seemed like an eternity since Vic had excused himself to go to the "little Vampires' room," and her guests were getting a bit ghoulishly grumpy.

"The hors d'oeuvres were delightful, dear," Valerie said. "But if I don't sink my fangs into some real food soon, I might just shrivel up and live."

"Yes, Vanna," Vernon said. "I'm so hungry, I could bleed a cow."

Just then the clock struck midnight. Vanna knew she could wait no longer. *Oh well,* she thought. *Vic will just have to wait for the drippings.*

She rang the silver bell next to her plate, which was the signal for the first course to be served.

As the sound of the bell faded away through the halls of her castle, Vanna smiled and looked toward the kitchen door. When it didn't open, her smile quickly became a snarl.

"Wait, let's—let's—let's talk, okay?" Curley Red stammered as he and Teacher Vic faced each other. They walked around and around in circles, never losing eye contact. Curley first tried to outglare Vic. Then he attempted to pull his gaze away. But when it came to Vampire powers, he was no match for Teacher Vic. Only Vanna and Vic's sister, Vivian, had ever beaten Teacher Vic in a staring contest. Curley Red wasn't much of a challenge.

"I know." Curley decided to try something his mom had told him before he was even old enough to fly: When in doubt, bribe. "I'll give you a dozen pints of my finest A positive if you'll let me go."

Teacher Vic's paralyzing stare never wavered.

"Okay." Curley felt his body starting to stiffen. "I'll throw in a quart of my private B negative."

Despite himself, Teacher Vic blinked. He hadn't had a good B negative in centuries.

"Ah, I see you're a negative man." Curley smiled. "If you're really nice, I'll make it a quart and a half."

Teacher Vic lowered his eyebrows and doubled his concentration.

Oh, pooh! Curley thought just before he was frozen solid in a hypnotic trance. *I knew I should have made it a half gallon.*

The split second Teacher Vic looked away from Curley, he heard the clock striking midnight and Vanna ringing the dinner bell.

Peter peeked through the keyhole and saw a snarling Vanna slowly rising from the table. "Vanna's coming!"

"What do we do now?" Donny said, shivering.

"We move fast." Teacher Vic could hear Vanna approaching. "Real fast. Grab that serving tray . . ."

Vanna's seat at the head of her seventy-foot-long table was at the far end of the room from the door to the kitchen. When there was no response to her ringing the dinner bell, she tried to remain calm. She attempted to stay cool as she rose from her seat. She fought to keep her composure as she floated slowly past her guests.

"Excuse me for a moment." Vanna smiled to the rows of drooling Vampires on either side of the table. "I'll just check on the delay in the kitchen. I'm sure it's just because Curley is whipping up some special surprise for us. He's such a playful little blood-biscuit."

Inside, Vanna was hotter than a volcano in Hades. *How dare he delay the meal,* she silently roared as she playfully patted Vance on the back and complimented him on his new outfit. *Embarrass me, will he? I'll have his fangs on a fork for this,* she raged internally while passing Veronica and happily congratulating her on her recent law degree.

Vanna nodded, laughed, and smiled to her guests as she approached the door to the kitchen. Her fury bubbled and boiled hotter with each inch she floated. With claws extended and fangs ready, Vanna reached the door, which suddenly opened and bopped her on the nose.

"Hot human coming through!" Amanda shouted.

Peter and Amanda came racing through the door, pushing a cart holding a huge serving tray with an enormous, shiny domed lid.

Vanna held her nose and hoped it wasn't bleeding. From the hungry look in her guests' eyes, she knew such an injury could have serious consequences.

"It's about time you got out here," Vanna whispered, and escorted Peter, Amanda, and the platter toward the table. "I hope you have something special under there." She drummed her claws on the dome.

"It's great." Amanda knew it would be wise to shut up and get this over with. However, silence had never been one of her strong points. "I just know you'll love it. I bet Curley Red has never been so *into* his work."

Amanda bit her tongue to avoid giggling, forgetting about the fact that she and Peter had hurriedly put their fangs back in place before coming out to put their plan into action. She must have cut herself slightly, because as soon as she bit down, each of the Vampires in the room either sighed loudly, growled noticeably, or fainted from the pleasure of smelling fresh blood. Fortunately everyone, including Vanna, thought the aroma originated under the dome.

"It does smell delicious." Vanna trembled slightly. "Do you really think Curley's outdone himself just for poor little me?" she asked in a voice loud enough for each of her guests to hear.

This time Peter answered, "Bet on it."

Deep in Vanna's private pantry, Laura started to shiver. Soon she started to shake with fear. As exhausted as she was, she wouldn't let herself close her eyes. She had made that mistake once and had instantly fallen asleep. She had dreamed she was a plucked turkey just before Thanksgiving. She was being chased by hundreds of Pilgrims. Not just ordinary Pilgrims. Pilgrims with fangs and glowing red eyes.

Now Laura's reality seemed much more frightening than any nightmare. She suddenly heard the sound of footsteps . . . footsteps that got louder

104

and louder until they stopped in front of the pantry door. A moment later the door flew open. To smother a scream, Laura bit into the sack that was covering her head.

All at once the footsteps resumed. This time they were inside the pantry. It sounded as if at least a dozen Vampires were scurrying from one corner of the room to the other, whispering her name. "Laura, Laura, where are you?"

These were the exact words spoken by the Pilgrims in her dream. She imagined herself being swarmed by Vampires. She blocked her ears. "Please don't let them find me," she prayed. "Please don't let them find me."

"I found her." The voice Laura heard was muffled by the sacks and her hands. She tried to roll herself into a tiny ball and disappear into the stone itself. She knew there was little or no chance of success.

"She's under these sacks!" the excited voice yelled. "You can see her breathing."

"Wait a minute," Laura said out loud. "I know that voice. It's . . ."

"Donny," Teacher Vic called from near the pantry door. "Get her and let's go."

Laura didn't wait for Donny to follow orders. She threw off the sacks, jumped up in the air, and kissed Donny on the way down. He stood dumbfounded.

"She kissed me!" Donny whispered over and over again as Laura slapped low, high, and medium behind-the-back fives with Amy and Gabe. She then ran to Vic and did something she'd never thought possible: She hugged a teacher.

"Don't get all human on me." Teacher Vic smiled. "You're not off the menu yet."

He wouldn't show it, but Teacher Vic was feeling pretty optimistic about the way things were turning out. As they raced back to the kitchen to collect the Three Frozen Stooges and two students, one thought kept going through Teacher Vic's mind—the plan was working.

But back in Vanna's dining room the future didn't look so bright. Peter and Amanda were supposed to simply deliver the platter and then return to the kitchen while Vanna said dis-grace. At all of her previous dinner parties Vanna had gone on for at least half an hour about how everyone should be very thankful that they had been invited. The food always made it worth the wait.

Teacher Vic had figured this would give them enough time to get Laura; come back for Peter, Amanda, Horace Easton, and the Drapers; and fly home without being noticed.

As *bad* luck would have it, Vanna selected this

particular dinner party to break the tradition. While Peter and Amanda wheeled the cart to the edge of the pool of candlelight surrounding the table, Vanna shortened her speech to a quick "Hooray, blood! Let's eat."

To the wild cheers of her guests, Vanna turned to Amanda and Peter and said those two little words so dear to any Vampire's heart: "Serve me."

Peter looked at Amanda. Amanda looked at Peter. They both looked at Vanna and said, "Huh?"

"Serve me," Vanna said, lounging back in her huge chair. *"Now!"*

Peter and Amanda knew they had no choice. Using all their strength, they lifted the platter off the cart. The two closest Vampires parted so that they could move it onto the table.

For true Vampire Scouts lifting the tray would not have been a problem. To Peter and Amanda it was as if they were trying to win the Olympic weight-lifting competition. Both strained all their muscles, held their breaths, and leaned in toward the platter.

Suddenly Veronica started to scream and screech.

Something had gone terribly wrong. Peter and Amanda's disguises were perfect. Everything from their fangs to the latest Vampire fragrance was in place. But there was one tiny thing Vic had forgotten.

Veronica pointed and shrieked, "The dome! Look at the dome!"

The other Vampires stared. Amanda's and Peter's very frightened faces were clearly reflected in the shiny silver surface for all to see. Shrill cries of madness and fury filled the room.

CHAPTER

"Run!" Peter howled. He and Amanda dropped the tray and ran. When they did, a three-quarters frozen Curley Red wearing black pajamas with moon bottoms tumbled to the ground. He looked half crazed and had a rotten apple stuffed into his mouth.

Vanna sat aghast. "Stop them!" she bellowed. "The Vampire that captures the food . . . drinks the food."

The Vampires leaped up from where they sat, causing about a hundred chairs to fall backward to the floor at the same time. There was a great *whoosh* as they flew into the air, prepared to swoop down on their prey. Vanna could see the joy in her friends' eyes. They had waited so long for the feeding frenzy to begin. Now, finally, they thought their unearthly appetites would be satisfied. They were wrong.

"Stop!" Vanna suddenly ordered in a voice so full

of evil that even the most vicious of her guests had no choice but to come to a screeching halt in midair.

Vanna knew there was no way her food could escape the castle, so why rush things? As the starving Vampires floated back down to the floor, Vanna giggled. She now realized that she could torture both her food and her guests at the same time. *What fun,* she thought. The food would have longer to think about being consumed, while her guests would have longer to wait to quench their agonizing thirsts.

Vanna smiled happily. "Let's make this a little sporting." She held up one hand like a police officer stopping traffic. "I will allow no flying."

Peter and Amanda heard the sound of Vampires groaning.

"You can only chase them on foot." Vanna paused before completing her new rules. "And you can only do it at human speed."

Peter and Amanda heard the sound of Vampires moaning.

"It's my party and they'll die when I want them to. Now I choose to play," Vanna said. "Oh, by the way, you'd better hurry before they get away."

Peter and Amanda heard the sound of many footsteps chasing after them.

The two humans darted for the kitchen door. Even with Vanna's rules and a head start there was absolutely no way they would have made it if Curley Red hadn't thawed out and stood up at the precise moment the lead Vampire, Vern, was stepping over him.

What followed was a collision that would be the top story on TV news programs and would make banner headlines in the evening papers across the V.K. Vampire slammed into Vampire, who slammed into Vampire, who slammed into Vampire. The news reporters would say investigators found the cause of the crash to be "human error."

While most of the Vampires tried to pull themselves from the wreckage and some talked to Veronica about suing for whiplash, Peter and Amanda made it out of the dining room, through the kitchen, and down several dark, twisting corridors. They didn't care where the corridors led, as long as they led . . . away.

Teacher Vic, Laura, Donny, Amy, and Gabe raced back toward the kitchen. Vanna's private pantry was all the way on the other end of the castle and inside a maze. They hadn't made it halfway back when they heard a loud crashing like that of many chairs dropping onto the floor.

Everyone thought the same thing at the same time. That thought was *Uh-oh*.

———

Within minutes, some of the Vampires regrouped and began to spread out through the castle in search of their prey. Driven by their unearthly hunger, each had the same goal: Find the fleeing food and begin to feast.

Teacher Vic never reached Amanda and Peter. Instead Amanda and Peter reached him. As Teacher Vic, Laura, Donny, Amy, and Gabe were taking a shortcut to the kitchen through Vanna's PowerCastle gym, Amanda and Peter came tearing in through another door and ran directly into their teacher. All three fell backward onto the hardwood floor.

Donny jumped forward, spread his arms out wide like a baseball umpire, and yelled, "Safe!" When no one laughed, giggled, or even smiled, he tried to talk his way out. "I mean, I'm glad you're all safe."

Amy put her hand over his mouth so that he wouldn't embarrass himself any further.

Amanda and Peter jumped to their feet; Teacher Vic floated into an upright position. "They're coming. All of them are coming," Peter said, panting.

"Vanna didn't say dis-grace. She wanted us to serve Curley." Amanda tried to catch her breath. "They saw our reflection. In the silver."

Teacher Vic slapped himself in the forehead, which can be a mistake if you have Vampire strength. After he again picked himself up off the floor, he groaned. "Reflections! I can't believe I forgot about reflections. Some teacher, huh? Duhhhhhhhhhhhh."

"Um, excuse me, Teacher Vic," Peter said. "But I think, maybe, we have bigger things to worry about right now."

The sound of a Vampire wailing somewhere in the castle convinced Teacher Vic that his student was absolutely correct.

"Who's in favor of going home?" Teacher Vic called for a show of hands.

Laura pulled on Teacher Vic's cape. "Excuse me, Teacher Vic," she said politely. "We can't go yet."

"Why not?"

"My dad and the Drapers. We can't just leave them behind."

"Details," Teacher Vic sighed. "I really hate details." He looked around Vanna's gym. Light from the full moon poured in from the two huge skylights, giving the gym an eerie glow. "Okay, wait for me over there, between the StareMaster and the stationary bites. I'll be right back."

For the first time that day, all the students sat down and relaxed. The break didn't last long. Almost as soon as Teacher Vic disappeared through one door, Vanna and the Vampires flew in through the other.

The students watched, frozen with fear, as the Vampires slowly floated toward them in the shadowy light. They were in a line that stretched across the gym. Some were growling; others just glared at them with pure hunger in their eyes.

"Remember, don't rush." Vanna showed her fangs. "I want you to build up your appetites to the point of pain, now that the menu has been expanded so nicely."

Several of the Vampires licked their lips.

"Plus, with this much food"—Vanna winked at the students—"the meal is now officially all-you-can-drink."

The students knew there was nowhere to run or hide. It also seemed highly unlikely that any argument, no matter how convincing, would convert the Vampires into vegetarians. Only one option remained: hold their ground and fight.

They stood up and faced the slowly approaching Vampire horde. Peter and Amanda took out their fake fangs and flung them at Vanna. Vanna caught them in one hand and squeezed them into dust. "Temper, temper. I'll take two with tempers to go." Vanna rubbed her belly. "I just love hot, spicy food."

Donny and Laura found some small weights on the floor and flung them at the Vampires. Vernon and

Veruca caught the weights like Frisbees and playfully tossed them through the far wall.

The Vampires were now only half a gym away and closing in slowly, very slowly.

"Okay, come on!" Peter shouted in defiance and took two steps forward. "Come and get us if you can."

"Yeah. You don't want to mess with us." Amanda joined him. "Uh-uh, you don't."

Laura, Gabe, and Amy joined their friends in making fists and issuing warnings.

For a moment the Vampires stopped moving in. They seemed somewhat taken aback by these brazen human actions until Donny joined in and said, "You guys hungry?" He did his impression of melting ice cream in a bowl, which he had first performed at a kindergarten talent show. "Well, how about some hot-blood sundaes?"

Donny had gone too far. No Vampire could ever resist dessert.

The Vampires all bared their fangs and again started to float toward the student buffet.

"Way to go, dweebacus." Gabe gave Donny a shove. "How did you ever make it to sixth grade?"

"Yeah," Peter said. "I bet he'd flunk gum chewing."

"Wait a minute," Amanda said as the Vampires closed in. "That's it!"

"What's it?" Donny asked.

"Quick," Amanda said. "Give me a piece of gum."

Teacher Vic flew into the kitchen just in time to pull Venessa's head back by her hair. Her fangs were at Horace Easton's throat, and she was about to quench her thirst.

The door to the dungeon was wide open. Horace had thawed out and released Venessa when she promised him a ride home and a quick bite. Horace thought she meant a snack at Wendy's. He didn't realize just how wrong he was until he felt the tips of her teeth on his Adam's apple.

"Back you go!" Teacher Vic tossed Venessa through the open dungeon door. She flew across the cell and landed in a crumpled heap against the far wall. Vic raced over and slammed and locked the dungeon door.

"Thanks," Horace said to Teacher Vic. "It's a good thing you got here. I might have hurt her. I had her right where I wanted her." Horace felt the two small round impressions Venessa's fangs had left on his neck. Suddenly he stopped bragging and hugged Teacher Vic with all his might. "Thank you, thank you, thank you, thank you, thank you."

Teacher Vic pulled away, a bit embarrassed by
Horace's enthusiasm. "Hurry." He lifted the domes
off of the Drapers, who had chosen to remain hidden
on their platters. "We have to get back to the gym
before it's too late."

Meanwhile, in the gym, it looked as if "too late" had
already arrived. Then Amanda demanded a last request.

"You want what?" Vanna sounded perplexed by
Amanda's plea.

"A last request," Amanda repeated. "We would
like to have one last piece of gum."

"It is not customary to grant food a last request."
Vanna thought about it. "But on the other hand, I
also like my meals to have a pleasant-smelling last
breath. Scent is so important to the sense of taste.
Very well, chew while you may."

"Donny," Amanda said, "please give everyone a
stick of gum."

"This is stupid," Donny said. "Who wants gum
now? Especially gum that tastes like—"

Amy put her hand over Donny's mouth.

"We all want gum," Peter said slowly. "Don't we,
Donny?"

Amy moved Donny's head up and down.

"We all especially want gum that tastes so

yummy," Amanda said. "The *Vampires* will just love the fresh way it smells, won't they, Donny?"

"How considerate," Vera said to Vlad, who just snarled and drooled.

Donny finally remembered the flavor of his trick bubble gum, and it dawned on him what Amanda meant. He nodded on his own and reached into his pocket. He gave each person a stick of gum.

Laura looked really confused, but she went along with the rest in unwrapping the gum and popping a piece into her mouth. As soon as the flavor assaulted the first taste bud, she knew why Amanda had made this particular last request.

The students enjoyed a few moments of pure chewing satisfaction before Vanna announced, "Enough!" She looked around at her fellow Vampires. "My dear guests." She pointed at the students. "Dinner is served."

The Vampires curled their lips back over their fangs and moved forward. The students puckered their lips and blew.

CHAPTER

Vlad was the first Vampire to suffer the consequences of poor table manners. He raced toward Gabe, determined to chugalug Gabe's contents before any other Vampire got even a single drop. Vlad saw Gabe blowing a bubble, but he didn't think much of it. After all, food often acted odd just before being eaten.

Gabe saw Vlad coming and turned to meet the attack. He blew his bubble so big that it actually blocked Vlad's path to his neck. With an evil laugh Vlad popped it with his left fang. Then Vlad fell backward, holding his face and screaming in pain.

"Garlic breath!" Vlad shrieked. "Garlic breath!"

When he'd bitten the bubble, the aroma of garlic gum had filled his mouth.

"Get it off me! Get it off me!" Vlad rolled on the floor, trying desperately to rub the thin coating of gum off his fang.

The other Vampires attacked, only to be driven off one by one by popping garlic bubbles.

"Take that!" Amy yelled as she blew a big one at Veronica, causing the dinner guest to cry out angrily and back away.

"Chew on this, batface!" Laura blew a bubble at Vernon, who knew she really didn't mean the compliment.

Valerie got a snootful of garlic when she tried to get to Peter's neck. Vernon chipped a fang when he dove for cover.

All the Vampires ran toward the back of the room, pursued by the gum-chewing, bubble-popping garlic brigade.

Bubble after bubble exploded its aromatic contents into the air. Vampire after Vampire fell to the floor, stunned by the unexpected assault on their senses.

Donny stood over Vanna. "Hey, guys, watch this." He bent down to blow a bubble directly into her face. He didn't notice that Vanna's eyes had suddenly cleared. As he blew a bubble and approached her nose, Vanna reached up and grabbed his throat, causing Donny's bubble to burst and cover his own face from nose to chin.

Vanna then floated up into the air, holding Donny over her head with her right hand. "Rise!" she called to her dinner guests. "Rise and dine!"

The students looked at each other in horror. "Quick," Peter said to Gabe, "smell my breath."

"Eat my shorts." Gabe looked away in disgust.

Peter cupped his hands over his own mouth and blew. He hoped his breath would smell like an explosion in a pizza palace. But when he breathed in, there wasn't even a hint of garlic. "Retreat!" he screamed. "The garlic's gone."

The students hadn't known one important fact about joke-garlic gum. The garlic flavor only lasted about five bubbles. By now all of them had blown their limit.

Vanna shook Donny in the air like a rag doll and growled. All at once she dropped him and started to giggle uncontrollably. Vanna was incredibly ticklish under her right arm. Teacher Vic knew her secret and had arrived just in time to tickle Donny free.

"Stop! Stop, Vic!" Vanna pulled away from Teacher Vic, who moved between his students and their would-be consumers.

Vanna stopped giggling. She moved to stand with her dinner guests, who were getting more impatient and hungrier with each passing moment. "I guess you know this means the engagement is off?" she snarled at Vic.

Teacher Vic nodded, smiled, and said, "But we can still be friends, can't we?"

Vanna answered with a hiss and a howl. She had never been so angry in her entire living death. It was bad enough that Vic had pretended to be her boyfriend. Now he was trying to free her food, thereby breaking the First Law. He was also completely destroying her evening and her reputation as the best party giver in the V.K. The whole thing was giving Vanna one killer of a headache.

It didn't help matters when Horace Easton and the Drapers, who had joined the group of students, stuck out their tongues and wiggled their ears with their hands. "Ha-ha-ha." Horace stuck out his chest and played the macho man. "Big tough Vanna couldn't suck a flea."

"Vanna is a wimpette. Vanna is a wimpette," Sam and Sammi chanted.

"Victor!" Vanna screamed. "You and your humans are as good as gulped."

Horace, Sam, and Sammi dove for the floor behind the students.

"Come on, Vanna," Teacher Vic said. "Cut the dramatics and let us leave—please."

"Silence, Victor. I don't think you fully understand your situation. You were invited to share my feast. Now you are destined to become part of it. You were going to break the First Law, but you failed. You are no longer one of us. You are one of them!" Vanna pointed to the students. "You were once magnificent. Now you're a munchie."

Vanna turned to her guests. "I call dibs on Victor. You can have the rest."

Vanna and the Vampires slowly started to move forward, but then they stopped dead in their tracks.

"Do you, like, have a problem, or what?" Vic's sister, Vivian, suddenly floated down through the ceiling and stood in front of her brother and his students. Vic's mom, dad, and brother, Vinnie, drifted down beside her.

"I'll say one thing about the V.K.," Peter whispered to Amanda. "They have great special effects."

"We're sorry to be late for your party, dear." Vic's mom touched Vanna's arm. "Traffic on the skyway was just deadly."

"Are we ever going to eat?" Vern whined. "We're starving."

"We eat now!" Vanna moved forward, but Vivian blocked her path. Vic and the rest of his family held their arms out, creating a cape wall between the dinner guests and the dinner.

"This is ridiculous." Veronica had had enough. "Sorry, Vanna, but I just can't wait any longer." She turned to the other guests. "I say we forget about this party disaster and go out for some Chinese." Beijing was one of Veronica's favorite cities.

"We had Chinese twice last week," Vance said. "Let's do Italian, or Mexican? Or Polish is nice."

"A bit heavy, don't you think?" Valerie said while pinching Vance's belly. "Perhaps French."

"That's too rich for my blood," Vernon said. "How about some Hungarian—goulashed. Or, I know, a nice Irish—stewed."

"Yum!" Valerie smacked her lips. "Do you know someone good?"

"The best." Vernon smiled.

"Then what are we waiting for?" Veronica clapped her hands wildly. "Let's go!"

Before Vanna could say a single word of protest, her dinner guests were gone. She heard Veronica's fading voice saying, "Next time you have a dinner, Vanna, I do hope you can control your food."

With her reputation in tatters and her dignity torn to shreds, Vanna was not in a very good mood. "I will destroy you all myself!"

Vanna moved to her right to get around Vivian, but instead of stepping aside, Vivian moved right along with her. Vanna moved to her left, and so did Vivian. Vanna tried up. Vanna tried down. But everywhere that Vanna went, Vivian was sure to go.

"You are so annoying," Vanna huffed.

"No kidding," Vivian's brother Vinnie said. "You should see her at home."

Vivian just smiled her oh so annoying sisterly smile and kept her position in front of Vanna.

Vanna moved forward, but once again Vivian blocked her way.

"Get out! Get out! Get out! Get out! *Get out!*"

"Chill, Van." Vivian smiled. "Don't you know that stress can kill?"

"So can I!" Vanna snarled.

Vivian snarled back.

Vivian's dad moved to his daughter's side. "Vanna, please," he said sincerely. "We've known you forever. I was at your first puncture. There is no doubt that you are a vicious, merciless, savage, stone-cold killer."

"Thank you." Vanna blushed.

"However, we just cannot allow you to harm Victor."

"But he's a teacher!" Vanna cried. "A teacher of *humans*."

"We're just as upset about that as you are, probably more. After all, he is our son. But it's for that very reason that we will not have him injured. Perhaps he'll change. You know what they say: Where there's death . . . there's hope."

After a long moment Vanna held up her hands and said, "Okay, you can take him home and get him some help. But leave the young humans to me."

Vic's dad turned to his son. "Sounds fair enough."

Teacher Vic folded his arms and frowned. "No way, no how, na-uh, forget it!"

"You can be so stubborn." Vic's dad turned back to Vanna. "Kids! Go figure."

"Okay, everyone," Teacher Vic called. "It's back on board the Vampire Express."

Once again Teacher Vic held Peter's hand on the right and Amy's on the left. As he'd done when they'd left the playground, he started to walk, pulling Peter's hand and gently pushing against Amy's. After a moment of confusion even Horace Easton and the Drapers caught on, and everyone in the circle was walking around and around. Then Teacher Vic quickened the pace.

"No!" Vanna screeched at the top of her lungs, causing the skylights and every window in the moon-lit room to explode outward.

Like a second merry-go-round gone mad, the group moved faster and faster until all was a blur. Then they started to rise.

"Stop!" At the sound of Vanna's voice the floors cracked and two walls crumbled.

Still the circle rose. The last thing Teacher Vic and his group heard before disappearing into the stars was Vanna screaming, *"No!* I will not allow this! You will never, *ever* escape!" And Vivian saying, "Sorry, Vanna-bo-banna, I think you might be mistaken."

The last thing they all saw was Vanna and Vivian charging at each other, their fangs flashing violently in the pale light of the moon.

They drifted past comets and around a million shooting stars. They flew through galaxies of golden glitter and sparkling silver seas. Then the flight abruptly ended in a cloud of dust and several very loud thuds.

"Oops!" the students heard Teacher Vic say. "Sorry about the hard landing, people. I must be getting a little rusty. But at least we're home."

When the dust cleared, six sixth-graders, three bewildered adults, and one teacher stood on the gravelly playground of Lincolnview School. While everyone cheered their safe return, Teacher Vic stumbled slightly. He felt an unusual tingling that started at his toes and raced up through every hair on his head. His jaws suddenly ached, and he couldn't stop blinking.

Teacher Vic convinced himself that these physical symptoms were a reaction to flying home with such a heavy load of passengers. However, he couldn't explain the nagging thought that kept popping into his mind. For the first time ever Teacher Vic had an incredible craving for a cheese sandwich, a bag of Doritos, and a nice Dr Pepper.

Laura was the first to notice that something about Teacher Vic had changed. Even though it seemed to be the middle of the day, he was making no effort to cover his head. Peter then saw that his skin was no longer ashen white, and Amanda watched as his gray eyes turned blue.

"Smile for us?" Amy asked.

"Why?" Teacher Vic smiled. His fangs were gone.

"You know all that First Law business?" Peter asked.

"Yeah?" Teacher Vic sounded a bit bewildered. He had a slight stomachache.

"Well, I think you've just been punished for breaking it. Look." Amy held a pocket mirror up in front of Teacher Vic's face. He saw his reflection and screamed.

"Who's there?" Teacher Vic twirled around, expecting to catch some stranger looking over his shoulder. The twirl made Teacher Vic dizzy, and he accidentally stepped on Peter's toes.

"Sorry, Peter. I was never so clumsy before."

"Don't worry about it." Peter smiled. "After all, you're only human."

———

For the next half hour everybody talked about their just-completed adventure while Teacher Vic prepared himself for the adventure he had just begun. Slowly he started to adjust to his new state of being. Soon, for the first time ever, Teacher Vic found himself actually enjoying what had become a beautiful sunny day.

"What time is it?" Amanda finally asked. "How long were we gone?"

Amy was shocked when she looked at her watch. Only an hour had passed since they'd left the playground for the V.K.

"Vampire time distortion," Teacher Vic explained. "When we flew home, we moved back in time. I must have already been losing some powers. I was hoping to make it back before we actually left. That way we could have told ourselves how things were going to work out."

"What?" Donny scratched his head.

"We'll talk about it in class," Teacher Vic said. "Right now I have to do something I always wanted to do."

"What's that?" Laura asked.

Teacher Vic smiled, threw off his cape, and rolled up his sleeves. "Work on my tan."

CHAPTER

The next Monday there was a big party in Room 113 at Lincolnview School. It was a redecorating party. Teacher Vic ordered one of every kind of pizza the nearby parlor had to offer, including one whole large pie with extra garlic just for himself. Peter liked sausage best; Amanda, double cheese; and Laura, pepperoni and mushrooms. Horace Easton and the Drapers were also invited to the party. They ate everything in sight, including the pie with double anchovies.

Lester and Frances flew around the room passing out napkins and complaining about their new working conditions. Both felt that being a human's helper was going to take some getting used to, but they were willing to give it a try.

The students got to vote on which radio station to listen to while they pulled the nails out of the window shades and let the sunshine stream in. The candles were stored in a big box. "Just in case there's ever a power failure," Teacher Vic said.

All the posters, except for one, stayed in place. Teacher Vic removed the *Phantom of the Opera* poster and replaced it with a full-length mirror. All day long he kept returning to the mirror. He'd stand there and stare at his reflection for minutes at a time. More than once he said things like "How do you think I'd look as a blond?" Or, "I don't know, maybe black isn't really my color."

It was a great day in what promised to be a great school year.

Over the next couple of weeks, everything went smoothly at Lincolnview School. In fact, nothing very unusual happened until one cloudy Tuesday evening.

Teacher Vic had just gotten into his new red Jeep after working late at school—it took him so much longer to grade papers now than it used to. All of a sudden Amanda, Peter, Laura, Donny, Amy, and Gabe came running around the school building screaming, "Teacher Vic! Teacher Vic! Wait!"

Teacher Vic reluctantly rolled down the driver's-side window. He, Lester, and Frances all wanted to get to their house in time to watch *Tales from the Crypt*. The TV show always reminded them of home. "What's all the excitement about?"

"There's a new teacher in Room 111," Peter said, still panting.

"So?" Teacher Vic said.

"We were talking to some of her students," Gabe said while trying to catch his breath.

"That's wonderful. I'm very glad you're making new friends." Teacher Vic started rolling up his window. Amanda stopped him.

"They told us she was really weird," she said, holding on to the window. "Really, really weird."

"Who isn't?" Teacher Vic tried prying Amanda's fingers off the window.

"Yeah," Laura said. "But they said her room is all dark, with candles."

"Allergic to light, maybe. Trust me, I understand." Teacher Vic knew he'd already missed at least the first five minutes of the program.

"She wears a cape," Donny said.

"Maybe she's just fashion-conscious."

Peter and Amanda spoke simultaneously. "Her name is Vivian."

Teacher Vic let go of Amanda's fingers. He was no longer in a hurry to get home.

Jerry Piasecki

CURLEY RED'S GUIDE TO A SUCCESSFUL VAMPIRE DINNER PARTY*
(*Human Edition*)

Hello, my human friends and munchables. This is my guide to a truly delightful Vampire dinner party. In light of the fact that this is the "Human Edition," certain changes have been made in the type of food to be prepared. However, follow these instructions and you'll be feeling like a fang-face faster than you can say "Neck nipping is nifty for naughty nanas, no?"

If you're interested in the Vampire Edition, just drop by my castle in the Vampire Kingdom around dinnertime. Remember, if you're human, I'm always ready to . . . serve you.

Good night and good eating.

Curley Red's—Caterer to the creatures of the night

CRYPT PREPARATIONS—WHAT EVERY
VAMPIRE PARTY PLANNER MUST KNOW

The proper atmosphere is vital to helping build your guests' unhealthy appetites. An extremely soft and

---

* Parental, Vampire, or Parental/Vampire guidance advised.

beautiful room setting is a chef's best friend. I suggest decorating your dining dungeon with any combination of the following items:

- Dead flowers. (For formal occasions—stems only.)
- Fresh weeds. (Scatter playfully about the room for best effect.)
- Black or red balloons (blown up).
- All other balloons (popped and strewn about).
- Black or red streamers (strung).
- Any other color streamers (crushed into balls or torn to shreds).
- Black tablecloth. (Paper, posterboard, towels, etc., can be used. Never entertain on a red tablecloth. If a Vampire should stop by and see a red covering, he will think dinner is over and that you are a very messy eater.)
- The darkest dinner plates possible. Each should have a staw on the left and a straw on the right.

Le Menu

(Remember, for best results, all items listed should be served at blood temperature.)

When planning a Vampire dinner human style, there is one important rule to remember: *The redder the better!* The Vampire delicacies listed below are followed by their translation into human terms:

- Veiny Surprise (Franco-American Spaghetti)— Serve on Ritz crackers. Suck spaghetti off cracker. Give cracker to birds.
- Pigeon Pâté on Toast (refried beans)—Slurp beans off toast. Give toast to birds.
- Blood Du Jour (tomato soup)—Lick bowl until dry. Give bowl to birds.
- Maggotroni and cheese (macaroni and cheese)— Cover with ketchup and enjoy. Forget about birds.
- Sloppy Joeys (Sloppy Joes)—Extra sauce, please.
- Brain Food (vanilla yogurt covered with strawberry sauce)—Looks as good as it tastes.
- Capillary Pie (strawberry or cherry pie)—Vanna's favorite, human style.
- Fangfurters (hot dogs)—Much ketchup required.
- Coagulated Quiche (strawberry cream cheese, bagel optional)—Real Vampires eat quiche.
- Blood Pudding (strawberry, raspberry, or cherry pudding)—Almost as good as the real thing.
- Pickled Plasma (red Jell-O)—Remember, straws only.
- Blood Berries Supreme (maraschino cherries)— Perfect for any occasion from formal dining to a simple transfusion.

- Artery Strips (red licorice)—These will really get the old blood flowing.
- Dumplings à la Dracula (meat ravioli)—Drop-dead delicious.
- Doughnuts of the Living Dead (jelly doughnuts)—Insert two straws and suck out contents. Only strawberry or raspberry jelly counts.
- Crypt Cocktail (strawberries, raspberries, cherries, and watermelon)—Mash together and stir until gross.
- Candied Corpuscles (red jelly beans)—Just like my great-grandVamp used to make.

BEVERAGES

Type O—Red Kool-Aid or Hawaiian Punch
Type A—Tomato juice or V-8
Type B—cranberry juice or red soda
Type AB—strawberry Quik or strawberry shake

Select any combination of these suggested menu items, or use your imagination. Remember, in preparing a proper Vampire feast creativity is crucial.

About the Author

Jerry Piasecki is the creative director for a Michigan advertising agency. Previously he was a radio newsperson in Detroit and New York. He has also written, directed, and acted in numerous commercials, industrial films, and documentaries. The writing he loves most, though, is for young readers, "where one is free to let the mind soar beyond grown-up barriers and defenses." Jerry lives in Farmington Hills, Michigan. He has a teenage daughter, Amanda, who has a dog named Rusty and a cat named Pepper.